SITUATION TRAGEDY

A Crime Novel

BY

SIMON BRETT

Futura

D1395831

A Futura Book

Copyright © Simon Brett 1981

First published in 1981 by Book Club Associates
By arrangement with Victor Gollancz Ltd

This edition published in 1986
by Futura Publications, a Division of
Macdonald & Co (Publishers) Ltd
London & Sydney

*All characters in this publication are fictitious and any
resemblance to real persons, living or dead, is purely
coincidental.*

All right reserved
No part of this publication may be reproduced, stored in a
retrieval system, or transmitted in any form or by any means
without the prior permission in writing of the publisher, nor
be otherwise circulated in any form of binding or cover other
than that in which it is published and without a similar
condition including this condition being imposed on the
subsequent purchaser.

0 7088 2582 6

Set in IBM Journal by 🅰\Tek-Art, Croydon, Surrey
Printed and bound in Great Britain by William Collins, Glasgow

Futura Publications
A Division of
Macdonald & Co (Publishers) Ltd
Greater London House
Hampstead Road
London NW1 7QX

A BPCC plc Company

TO THE PEOPLE WHO
TAUGHT ME THE VALUE
OF TELEVISION,
WITH GRATITUDE

'TELEVISION: A medium, so called because it is
neither rare nor well done.'

Ernie Kovacs

CHAPTER ONE

The cast didn't see the opening titles for West End Television's new situation comedy until just before the Dress Run on the day of the pilot recording in January. Even the Director and Producer hadn't seen the final version till then. The titles were animated and, as every television Cost Planner in the world insists on saying lugubriously at every budget meeting he attends, animation is expensive and takes time. (From the point of view of the cast, the animated titles were a strong encouragement. A pilot show of uncertain future would often be prefaced by a cheap mock-up from Graphics, played over music from disc. The fact that West End Television had invested in animation and had commissioned a special signature tune by none other than Carl Anthony, composer of *Lumpkin!* and other hit musicals, suggested more than tentative confidence in the new project.)

The animation showed cartoon figures of a tweeded Colonel and wispy wife on a golf course. The flags in the holes of the distant greens were Union Jacks. The tweeded Colonel thrashed and puffed bad-temperedly at the ball, while his wispy wife carried his clubs and seemed sweetly to offer unwelcome advice. Carl Anthony's music, though played on steel guitars and synthesisers, had the blimpish overtones of military marches.

Over this pleasing charade, the following words appeared, in varied sizes of type (which had been the subject of earnest discussion between the agents of the various artists involved and the Casting Director who negotiated their contracts):

AURELIA HOWARTH
GEORGE BIRKITT
in

THE STRUTTERS

by
Rod Tisdale

with
BERNARD WALTON
and
Nick Coxhill
Debbi Hartley

These last two, likely to play regular parts in any ensuing series of *The Strutters*, had shrewd agents, who had insisted on their clients being billed at the beginning of the show.

Charles Paris, who would play the regular part of Reg, the golf club barman, in any ensuing series of *The Strutters*, had as his agent one Maurice Skellern, who was so surprised at the prospect of his client being in potentially regular and lucrative employment that he hadn't thought to ask about billing.

Most of the cast were clustered in the audience seats of Studio A at W.E.T. House, watching the titles on the large eidophor screen suspended above them. As the music faded and the screen went blank, Bernard Walton rose to his feet. 'I see,' he commented shortly. 'If I'm wanted, I'll be in my so-called dressing room, Number Three.'

'What's got up his nose?' Charles Paris asked George Birkitt, who was sitting beside him.

'Doesn't like the billing, I imagine.'

'Why? What's wrong with it? He can't surely expect to be above you and Aurelia. It's your show, after all.'

'No, he wouldn't want that. He just probably thinks he should be above the title or have a "Special Guest Appearance" tag. No doubt he thinks the word "with" is demeaning for someone of his stature.'

'God, it must be awful to have to worry about things like that.'

'Ah well, when you're a Star, it's important. You can't afford to let your status slip.'

'Hmm. I don't think I'll ever have that problem,' said Charles Paris, with his customary accurate assessment of his own position in the theatrical hierarchy. He felt mellow. The price of alcohol was pleasingly subsidised in the West End Television bar. Four glasses of red wine, and a couple of large Bell's to settle them, had slipped down very comfortably. Have to have a pee before the Dress Run starts, he thought lazily.

Once you got used to the pace of television, he found, it was quite pleasant. Once you realised it was just unremittingly slow and that there was lots of hanging around. Of course, it'd be different if you had a big part, if you had to stand around in character all the time they rearranged their cameras, repositioned their sound-booms, and titivated set and costumes. Then you might be affected by the pervading atmosphere of bad temper and barely suppressed panic characteristic of television studios. But when you were playing Reg, the golf club barman, when you had mastered your fourteen lines and two moves during a lazy week of morning rehearsals, and when you had got four glasses of red wine and two large Bell's inside you, you could drift serenely through, unaffected by your environment.

George Birkitt, considering he was about to record his first starring television performance, also seemed commendably relaxed and sensible. He picked up Charles's remark. 'No, heaven forbid. All that star business is just not worth the aggravation.'

'Will you say the same when *The Strutters* is top of the ratings and you can't go into a pub without people saying, "Ooh, look, it's Colonel Strutter"?'

'I'll face that problem when I come to it,' said George with a grin. 'Anyway, there's many a slip, and all that. I've been in too many shows that were going to change the course of theatrical history and then closed after one night, to get too excited about this.'

'Oh, come on, you must have got a frisson when you saw those titles, your name at the top with Aurelia. Must mean something.'

'Not a lot. "Men are led by toys" — I think Napoleon said that.' George Birkitt shrugged non-committally, but there was a gleam of childlike excitement in his eye. Afraid it was too transparent, he changed the subject. 'Perhaps you ought to go and calm Bernard down. He's your friend, isn't he?'

'Hardly,' said Charles, though it was a difficult question to answer. He had known Bernard Walton quite well when the young man had started his theatrical career, and indeed in a production of *She Stoops to Conquer* in Cardiff ('Somewhat leaden-footed' — *Western Mail*) Charles had been the first director to make a feature of the natural stammer which was now such a popular butt of impressionists. But as Bernard Walton's career had shot upwards, he had moved into a rather different league from his former mentor. Charles was quite content that this should be so, since he had never felt a great affinity for the young man, and certainly no affinity for the glamorous, social side of showbusiness in which he now moved. Bernard, however, would occasionally swoop down on Charles with embarrassingly patronising invitations or offers. Charles usually avoided the invitations, feeling, not without justification, that he would only be paraded as evidence of the star's common touch and proof of how loyal he remained to old friends. The moment Charles dreaded was the inevitable one when Bernard became the subject of *This Is Your Life*, and once again wheeled out the old chum from Cardiff to testify to his genuine, unspoiled nature. Gestures like keeping Charles in tow, the charity work he did with handicapped children, fundraising for the Variety Club and Lords' Taverners (all discreetly leaked to the press by his Publicity Manager), together with comments in the *Sun* about the return of the mini-skirt and descriptions of his favourite pudding in the *TV Times*, ensured that the public was constantly aware of the sheer loveability of Bernard Walton.

On the other hand, though Charles Paris could, and usually did, balk at the social invitations, he never turned down any work that came his way through Bernard. In fact, he hardly ever turned down any work from any source. His was not a career of constant decision, weighing the advantages and disadvantages of one job against another; it was a career of grabbing whatever he was offered quickly, before anyone changed their minds.

And so, when he discovered that Bernard Walton, star of West End Television's hit sit. com., *What'll the Neighbours Say?*. had recommended him for the tiny part of Reg, the golf club barman, in one episode of the series, Charles had had no hesitation in accepting it. He was not then to know, and nor was his magnanimous sponsor, that the success of the minor characters, Colonel and Mrs Strutter (played by George Birkitt and Aurelia Howarth), would be so great that they would be promoted from Bernard's neighbours and sidekicks into the stars of a new spin-off series called *The Strutters*. And that, because of the convenience of the golf club bar for linking scenes (and because the company saw an opportunity to save the expense of a new set), Reg the golf club barman would be a regular character in the new series (if it passed the test of the pilot currently in the studio).

Bernard Walton had condescended to take a guest part, as his old *What'll the Neighbours Say?* character, just for the first episode of the new show, to provide a link for the audience and speed the setting up of the new situation, but he had expected more recognition of his generous gesture. Not just to be dismissed with a 'with'. Nor to be demoted from Dressing Room One, traditionally his on *What'll the Neighbours Say?* recording days, to make way for the recently promoted Aurelia Howarth who, whatever her achievements in a long stage career, had not, to Bernard's way of thinking, anything like his stature in television.

A deeper anxiety, not spoken out loud but hinted at by the cast of *The Strutters*, may also have affected Bernard Walton's state of mind. Though West End Television had an option on dates for a further series of *What'll the Neighbours Say?*, they seemed slow in taking it up. Rumour had it that the Company's Director of Programmes, Nigel Frisch, was waiting to see how the public reacted to the spin-off before making a final decision on the parent show.

Which posed a considerable threat to the career of Bernard Walton.

Charles Paris was aware of all this as he talked to George Birkitt about the threatened star. So too was George Birkitt. When Charles had declined the suggestion that he should smooth Bernard's ruffled feathers, saying it was the producer's job, since producers must make themselves useful *sometimes*, George commented, 'Pity about the dressing room, though. It would have been easier if they'd put me in Number One.'

Responding to Charles's raised eyebrow, he hastened to correct the false impression. 'No, no, I'm not getting big time. I just mean that I could have pretended there was some mistake and done a discreet swap with Bernard. I don't mind having Three. Whereas, Aurelia . . . By the time you've got that old dear safely installed, it'd be cruelty to move her. And by the time she's got Cocky settled, it'd be impossible.'

Cocky was a singularly revolting, aged Yorkshire terrier belonging to Aurelia Howarth. He was said to have been named after the impresario, C. B. Cochran, one of whose 'Young Ladies' the actress had been.

'Anyway, the dressing rooms aren't our problem,' said Charles, recapturing the Olympian detachment of the slightly drunk.

'Suppose not. Who sorts out who gets which?'

'I think the PA does a list.' It was likely. Production Assistants are responsible for a surprising range of duties in television.

'Ah, the lovely Sadie.' George Birkitt grimaced.' Well, I wouldn't be surprised if she were deliberately trying to antagonise Bernard. She really seems to enjoy making trouble. Do you know what she said to me this morning?'

'No,' Charles fed obligingly.

'She said, "Enjoy your brief day of stardom — it's the only one you're likely to get." '

'Charming.'

'Yes, I don't think I've ever met anyone with quite her knack for being gratuitously insulting. I mean, what she said may well be true, but it's not the sort of thing an actor welcomes first thing in the morning on a studio day.'

'No. I think she gets her name from her direct lineage from the Marquis de Sade.'

George Birkitt chuckled politely. There was a pause. He looked at his watch. For the first time he betrayed signs of nervousness. 'If we don't start soon, we're not going to get in a Full Dress Run.'

'What is the time?'

'Nearly five to five. We were meant to start at quarter to. They'll stop at six, however far we've got.'

'Oh, they'll let us finish if —'

'No, they won't. Got to have their forty-five minutes to line the cameras up, and then their hour's meal-break. Union rules. Actually they'll stop on the dot tonight. There's a union meeting a six. In the Carpenter's Shop or somewhere. It was announced over the speakers at lunch — didn't you hear it?'

6

'No, I . . .'

'So maybe all our efforts will be in vain. If they call a strike, the show won't get made.'

'That likely?'

'No, I think we'll be all right tonight. But there'll be trouble soon. I've got friends in the know who say all the ITV companies could be out by the summer.'

'What, because the BBC had just got a pay award?'

George Birkitt nodded.

'Yes, of course,' observed Charles Paris sagaciously. 'The BBC went on strike to achieve parity with ITV, so it's only a matter of time before ITV goes on strike to achieve greater disparity from the BBC.'

At this moment the object of their earlier odium, Sadie Wainwright, the PA, appeared on the studio floor from the Production Control. She was tall, blonde and attractive in a thin-lipped way. Her tan seemed to be permanent, as if in homage to her South African origin. She was neatly dressed in beige cord trousers and a flowered shirt. Gold chains clunked round her neck and wrists. She moved purposefully, clutching a pile of white camera cards.

In her wake, hesitant but not daunted, came the trainee PA who was trailing her. At outside rehearsals, where Charles had first registered that she was rather attractive, he had discovered that her name was Jane Lewis. By contrast to Sadie, her skin was almost white, sprinkled with tiny freckles. Her eyes were water-colour blue, but their paleness, together with that of her face, gained distinction from the defiant blackness of her hair, which was centrally parted and cut short.

Sadie made a considerable production of handing out the white cards to the cameramen. 'The director,' she pronounced, ladling contempt on to the word, 'has changed so many shots in that Sitting Room scene that I've just had to type all these out or you'll never find your way around.'

As she did her tour, she was followed by a tall angular figure in pale green trousers and sympathetically green striped shirt. This was Mort Verdon, the Stage Manager, who was in charge of the outside rehearsals and the organisation of props and a thousand and one other small duties around the studio. One didn't have to see the diamond stud in his ear or hear the swooping drawl of his voice; his every movement had the desired effect of advertising his proud overt gayness.

As he followed behind Sadie, he kept trying to get her attention. 'Sorry, boofle. Sorry, lovely. Quick whisper, eh?'

When she had distributed all her cards, he got his quick whisper. But, though he may have wanted to be discreet, she had no such desire. When she'd heard Mort's request, she snapped, 'No, of course we can't do anything about the dressing rooms at this stage. He'll have to lump it.'

Another fluttering whisper.

'No, the bloody dog has to stay there. Now can we get on with this bloody wake?'

The Floor Manager, a hearty young man called Robin Laughton, who had ambitions to direct, took this as a cue for the start of the dress run. 'Okay, boys and girls, let's have a bit of hush. We are in a Dress Run situation. Can we have all the artistes for —'

'Not yet!' blazed Sadie Wainwright. 'I'm not in the box. You can't start till I'm in the box.'

'But Scott says —' Robin Laughton gestured ineffectually to the earpiece which kept him in direct communication with the director in Production Control.

'Sod Scott! You can't start till I'm in there to do the count-down.'

'Scott says we're pushed for time.'

'And if we are, whose bloody fault is that? What do you expect with directors who don't know what they're doing? Scott Newton — huh. He couldn't direct piss into a pot.'

This colourful invective impressed the studio into silence. The cast stopped muttering in the audience seats. The cameramen disengaged themselves from their cameras. The sound-boom operators hung expectant from their mobile platforms. The assembled throng of scene-shifters, painters, carpenters and men whose only function seemed to be to wear lumberjack checked shirts, suspended their discussion of racing and overtime rates. The dressers stopped bitching and the make-up girls arrested their powder-puffs.

Only one man seemed unaware of the atmosphere. Rod Tisdale, author of many television comedy gems, including *What'll the Neighbours Say?* and *The Strutters*, stepped out of the shadows towards Sadie. He was a man totally without distinguishing features, so ordinary as to be indescribable. The only thing that distinguished him from the archetypal man in the street was the huge amount of money he made from his well-tried writing formula. But since he never spent any of it, even the money was hardly distinctive.

'Sadie,' he said in his toneless voice, 'while there's a lull . . . I wonder if you could just give a note to Scott. In the Estate Agent's Office scene, I think it'd be better if the Colonel said, "Not in these trousers", rather than "Not in this suit".'

'What?' demanded Sadie scaldingly.

'Should have thought of it before,' Rod Tisdale continued, impervious and without inflection. 'Old rule of comedy — suits aren't funny, trousers are. See what Scott thinks.'

'Suits, trousers — what does it matter?'

'Oh, it matters a lot, Sadie. One's a joke, one isn't.'

'Well, don't bother me with it. Tell your "joke" to little Jane. Maybe she'll write it down in her immaculate shorthand — there must be something she can do.' Sadie turned to leave, but thought of one more parting shot. 'Maybe sometime, Rod, you'll point out the other jokes in this script to me — I was damned if I could see any!'

And she stalked off majestically to the Production Control. The atmosphere relaxed. Charles Paris suddenly was again aware of how much he wanted to do a pee.

But too late. Robin Laughton leapt forward on a cue from his earpiece and cried, 'Okay, we are in a Dress Run situation. We'll take the opening titles as read to save time, and go straight to the Sitting Room scene. Strutters and Removal Men — Okay? And it's only a short scene, so stand by in the Golf Club Bar.'

Oh damn, thought Charles, have to use a bit of self-control.

George Birkitt and Aurelia Howarth took up their opening positions outside the Sitting Room door. On the set the two Removal Men, played by a couple of those character actors who are never out of work, prepared to deliver Rod Tisdale's computerised jokes.

'Okay, bit of hush,' bellowed Robin Laughton. 'This is a Dress Run situation. Good luck, boys and girls. Imagine titles, music, dum-de-dum-de-dum — and CUE!'

'Hey, Fred,' said the First Removal Man looking at a cut-glass decanter with a gummed label on it, 'What does F-R-A-G-I-L-E mean?'

But before the Second Removal Man could say, 'I don't know. Chuck it over here and I'll have a look', a new figure bounded on to the studio floor, and, with a cheery cry, ensured that they had to start again.

It was Peter Lipscombe, the show's boyish producer.

'Hello, everyone,' he said. 'Everything okay?'

In spite of their earlier anxiety, they completed the Dress Run in good time. One of the reasons why Rod Tisdale made so much money out of his scripts was that they were always very simple technically. Scott Newton, as a new young director with aspirations, had planned all kinds of clever shots over shoulders, through flower vases and looking down from cranes, but as rehearsals progressed, it had become clear that there was only one way to shoot a Rod Tisdale script, and that was to follow the predictability of the jokes. So the camera script had become a sequence of three linked shots — MCU (Mid-Close-Up) of Character A setting up joke, MCU of Character B delivering pay-off, CU (Close-Up) of reaction from Character A to milk audience laughter. Very little else was needed.

So they finished at five to six, having played their show to the sycophantic laughter of the producer, the Casting Director (a dramatic ex-actress called Tilly Lake) and the warm-up man, a minor comedian called Charlie Hook, whom Charles Paris remembered, though with little warmth, from a previous pilot he had made for West End Television, *The New Barber and Pole Show*.

Scott Newton bustled out of the Production Control at five to six, with Sadie Wainwright in tow, and Jane Lewis punctiliously following her. 'Right, a few notes,' he said rather feebly.

He didn't look well. The day was proving a strain and he patently wasn't getting the moral support a director can usually count on from his PA. He had only been freelance for about six months, having left a cosy niche in BBC Schools Department for the higher earning potential of the commercial world. Like many others of his age in television, he had recently been divorced, and was finding that the demands of maintenance payments inhibited the glamorous life-style he thought appropriate to a young television director.

The Strutters was his first big show, and he didn't appear to be enjoying it. 'A few notes,' he repeated with even less conviction.

'Okay, boys and girls,' Robin Laughton bellowed, as if testing a famous, but distant, echo. 'We are in a note-giving situation. Could all artists assemble in the Sitting Room set.'

Damn. Charles Paris had been half way out of the studio door on his way to the Gents. Reluctantly, he came back. The pressure on his bladder was almost intolerable.

The cast assembled with indifferent grace in the Sitting Room set. 'Right now, notes,' said Scott Newton slowly.

'Come on, hurry up,' urged Sadie. 'I've got a lot to do. And we'll have to get out of the studio when they start the Line-up at six.'

'Okay, okay, sure. Now, notes. George and Aurelia, in that first scene —'

Peter Lipscombe bounded up again, Tigger-like. 'Hello, everything okay?'

'Yes, yes, fine, thank you, Peter. Just giving a few notes. Er, George and Aurelia, in that —'

'Sorry, love,' interrupted Robin Laughton. 'Can we release cameras and sound? Sound Supervisor just asked me. They've got this union meeting.'

'Yes, sure. Um, George and Aurelia, could you —'

'Oh, I can't wait while you dither around,' snapped Sadie. 'I've got to go and give Telecine all the revised cues. Here are the notes.' She thrust a clipboard at Scott and marched off.

Charles saw his opportunity. What had been an urgent need was now an absolute necessity. 'Just got to nip to the Gents. Be back in a —'

'I'm not surprised, the amount you drink,' Sadie tossed savagely over her shoulder, as she barged out of the studio.

'Okay, Charles,' said Scott Newton, thought there was no chance of the actor waiting for permission. 'We'll continue notes in the Control box if we have to move out of here . . .'

Charles Paris moved swiftly across the studio, trying not to break into the indignity of a run. As he went, he heard

11

Scott continue, 'Now, George and Aurelia —'

'Scott darling,' fluted Aurelia Howarth's cultured elderly voice, 'I am a little worried about Cocky. The poor darling's in the Quick Change Room. I wonder if . . .'

'Yes, just a —'

'Okay, boys and girls,' bellowed Robin Laughton. 'Six o'clock. We are in a Line-up situation. Clear the studio.'

After the blessed relief of the Gents, Charles splashed water from the basin over his face. Sober up a bit before the next onslaught. It was a long break, an hour and three-quarters, before they were due to start recording. And that would inevitably mean one or two more drinks.

He looked at himself in the mirror. Dressed in the golf club blazer selected by Wardrobe, he looked more respectable than usual. Not in bad nick really for a man of fifty-two. And in work. In work! With the strong possibility of more work. Life felt good.

He walked out of the Gents and started instinctively towards the bar. Sadie Wainwright, in a rare moment of charity, had shown him a quick way up a fire escape on the outside of the building, which avoided waiting for slow lifts. He started up the metal steps, thinking what a flimsy structure it was on the outside of a comparatively modern block. He looked down to the car park some forty feet below.

He was half way up before he remembered the notes. Of course, he must remember that being in work did involve actually doing the job as well as drinking amiably in the bar. He started back down the metal fire escape.

The Production Control box was empty when he got there. All the banks of monitor screens were either blank or showing test cards. There was no one visible through the glass to the left in Vision Control, or to the right in Sound Control. They must be doing the notes elsewhere.

As he turned to go, he heard a voice clearly from one of the speakers. It was a familiar voice, recognisable from its South African twang, and even more recognisable from its tone of contempt.

He only heard two sentences, before the Sound Controller appeared in the box to his right and switched off the sound.

The two sentences were: 'You couldn't kill me. You haven't got it in you.'

CHAPTER TWO

'Everything okay, Charles?' asked Peter Lipscombe from his position at the bar.

'Fine thanks.' Then, feeling that some comment was required, Charles offered the opinion that the recording had gone all right.

The producer confided that he thought it was very exciting, but very exciting. That wasn't exactly the word Charles would have used for the evening but, since the next question was what he would like to drink, he didn't discuss it. The importance of most things diminished when he had a large Bell's in his hand.

Because he had only been in costume above the waist (barmen always being shot with their bottom half obscured by the bar), because he hadn't bothered to remove his make-up, and because he knew the short cut up the fire escape, Charles had managed to be the first of the cast to arrive in the bar. (He didn't pride himself on many abilities, but, in all modesty, had to recognise that he had few rivals in speed of getting to bars after performances.) He sat down with his drink and watched the rest of the actors and crew assemble.

As he did so, he witnessed a transformation of Peter Lipscombe. Whereas during the week of rehearsal the producer had been little in evidence and, when present, unobtrusive and diffident, he was now showing real dynamism in the business of taking people's orders for drinks and putting them through to the barman. Charles wondered whether he had finally answered a question that had puzzled him in all his previous dealings with television comedy. While the director's function, taking rehearsals and organising cameras, was obvious, what on earth was the producer there for? Peter Lipscombe's proficiency as a waiter suggested that at last the function had been explained.

'I think you may have to cope with a success for the first time in your life, Charles.'

13

The actor looked up to the familiar voice and saw the perfectly groomed figure of his friend Gerald Venables. He had forgotten that the solicitor had asked for a ticket for the recording. Though they had first met at Oxford in the OUDS, for whom Gerald had been an assiduous and commercially successful treasurer, he had never shown much interest in Charles's subsequent theatrical career, except when it involved television. The actor secretly believed that this was because commercial television was the medium whose values were closest to Gerald's own — those being that the sole aim of the arts is to make as much money as possible. The solicitor had certainly followed this tenet in his own show-biz practice, which was one of the reasons why he always walked around looking like the ideal executive in an American Express advertisement. On this occasion he favoured a dark blue double-breasted suit with a nuance of a chalk stripe, a blue-and-red paisley silk tie, and black patent-leather shoes restrained by a redundant strip of metal. The silver hair was trendily coiffed, and the tan would suggest to the uninitiated regular winter use of the sunlamp, but to those who knew Gerald's habits, a recent return from skiing in Verbier.

Charles, now back in his customary sports jacket (described once by a fellow actor as 'a sack with an identity problem'), reflected again on the incongruity of the friendship, as he offered Gerald a drink.

'No, I'm fine, thanks. Just been talking to the Head of Contracts and he bought me one.'

'And you really think this show'll work?'

'Oh, absolutely. It has all the hallmarks of a successful situation comedy.'

'What, you mean total witlessness, exaggerated performances and the perpetuation of harmful prejudices?'

'Now, Charles, you must curb your cynicism. Not only does this offer you more chance of making money than you've ever had in your so-called career, it is also a perfectly adequate, well-crafted and well-cast little show, which should be good for at least three series.'

'Sorry, I can never judge this sort of comedy. Enumerate its virtues for me, would you?'

'Okay. One, it's a good, simple situation — old fogey from the days of Empire, discipline, National Service, etc.

14

reacting to the slackness of modern life. Two, the script has jokes in the right places and in the right frequency.'

'But they're pretty old ones.'

'That doesn't matter. Audiences like recognition. Old jokes make them feel cosy. Three, it has a very good cast. George Birkitt is a real find. I think that crusty pig-headedness could catch on just like Alf Garnett. The rest of the cast is perfectly adequate . . .'

'Thank you,' said Charles with some acidity. The word had unfortunate associations for him. One of the high-spots of his theatrical career, his performance of a major Shakespearean role at Colchester, had been hailed in the *Eastern Daily Press* with the sentence, 'Charles Paris provides an adequate Macbeth.'

Gerald continued, unperturbed, 'What is more, the show has a secret ingredient, that little spark of magic which will raise it from the ranks of the commonplace.'

'What's that?'

'It has Aurelia Howarth, my childhood idol. And, though it would have hurt me to admit it at the time, she was not just *my* idol. The whole country was in love with her — and always has been. Right from those revues back in the Twenties — which, before you make any snide remarks, I was too young to see. But then with all those wonderful movies in the Thirties, and all her work during the war and . . . and everything. She's absolutely inspired casting. Who thought of her? Was it the producer?'

'I shouldn't think so. Mind you, he's probably capable of buying her a drink.'

'Anyway, as I say, I think you're on to a winner.'

Charles Paris smiled, gratified. 'Well, I hope you're right. And thank you very much for coming to see me.'

'Oh, I didn't come to see *you*,' said Gerald Venables. 'I only came because I thought you could introduce me to Aurelia Howarth.'

At that moment the object of the solicitor's adoration appeared at the main entrance to the bar. (Charles noticed with satisfaction that nobody else seemed to know about the short cut up the fire escape.)

In describing Aurelia Howarth, it was impossible to avoid the word 'well-preserved'. Though she was of the

the generation who thought it impolite to define a lady's age with too much precision, sheer logic and a knowledge of her theatrical achievements made it impossible for the most gallant admirer to put her birth much later than 1904, which made her at least seventy-five when the pilot of *The Strutters* was recorded. But, with the help of skilled couturiers and a lifetime's practice of make-up, she carried her years gracefully. Even as she entered the bar, encumbered by a huge bouquet under one arm and the odious Cocky under the other, her poise did not desert her. Though she had none of the egocentricity of the prima donna, she could never help making an entrance. Now she paused in the doorway, as if anticipating the applause of recognition. It was not a calculated gesture, just something that was instinctive to her.

She still had the slightness so familiar from early publicity photographs, and still enhanced it by wearing dresses skilfully draped about with diaphanous hangings. These, together with an aureole of pale golden hair (surely not natural, but so subtly coloured as to deny artifice), gave her a blurred outline, as if she was always viewed through soft focus. The skin of her face still had a softness, probably the result of a lifelong application of skin creams, and, though it sagged a little round her eyes and neck, remained commendably taut, but without that synthetic shininess which is the legacy of facelifts.

The eyes retained the pure blue clarity which had been remarked by Sacha Guitry, Jack Buchanan and Noël Coward, and the unfocused, abstracted stare which the pre-war public had found so sexy. They reinforced the aura of charming vagueness, which her manner of speech did nothing to dispel.

She did not have to wait long in the doorway for her appearance to register. Peter Lipscombe gambolled across from the bar, asked, 'Everything okay, Aurelia?' and took her order for a drink. At a slower pace, a very elderly man inched towards her and greeted her effusively.

He was eccentrically dressed in a blue blazer with an elaborate heraldic badge, and what appeared to have been white cricket flannels. His black shoes had the highly polished gloss of a previous generation. An open white flannel shirt revealed a blue, yellow and green cravat, fixed with a pearl-headed pin. The looseness of the cravat accentuated the thinness of a tortoise neck, on which an almost hairless head bobbled uneasily. Face and hands showed the stark contours of the bone beneath, their flesh eroded by the steady wash of age.

'Good Lord, it can't be,' murmured Gerald.

'Can't be what?' asked Charles.

'I think it is, though.'

'Who?'

'It must be.'

'Will you stop being bloody oracular and tell me who it is.'

'Barton Rivers.'

'That's a vaguely familiar name.'

'Aurelia's husband. I thought he must be dead by now. He's nearly ninety, must be. I met him at some charity dinner ten years ago and he seemed so doddery and gaga, I thought he couldn't last long *then*.'

'They've been married for ever, haven't they?'

'Pretty well. It's always hailed as one of the great show-biz marriages, giving the lie to all those generalisations about show-biz marriages. No, they must have been married in the early Twenties, because I seem to remember they had a son who was old enough to get killed in the war.'

'Barton was an actor, wasn't he?'

'Oh yes, you'll see his face in bit-parts in pre-war British films. Did the revue circuit too. Even wrote a bit, I think. Never as successful as she was, and didn't seem to do anything after the war.'

'Ah.'

'Anyway, come on, what are you hanging about for? Introduce me.'

'Gerald, I can't.'

'Yes, you can.'

When he approached her, he received the full benefit of the misty blue eyes and a throaty, 'Charles, darling.'

'Lovely performance tonight, Aurelia.' It wasn't his usual style, but somehow the old actress's charm seemed to demand it.

'Do call me "Dob", darling,' she cooed. She had always

17

been known as 'Dob' in the business, but Charles wouldn't have dared to use it without her express permission.

Even with it, he had difficulty in bringing himself to say the name. 'Thank you . . . er . . . Dob. I'd like, if I may, to introduce you to a friend of mine, who's always been one of your greatest fans.' Charles hated doing things like this. 'Gerald Venables . . . this is . . . er . . . Dob Howarth.'

Gerald took her hand and kissed it gallantly, which was just the sort of thing he would do. Aurelia seemed charmed by the gesture and favoured the solicitor with the beam of her eyes, which still, in spite of her age, remained surprisingly sexy. 'I'm enchanted to think that someone as young as you should remember an old lady like me.'

Gerald glowed predictably, like a schoolboy who had won a prize. Charles tried to work out why he didn't find the exchange as sickening as he did most show-biz syco-phancy, and decided it was because Aurelia Howarth was a genuinely warm person.

'But, darlings,' she continued, 'I haven't introduced you to my dear old boy, have I? This is Barton Rivers, my adorable husband . . . and this is Charles Paris, whom you saw in the show as our barman . . . and Gerald Venables.'

Charles was impressed by the way she had got the names exactly right. He also felt, through the theatrical hyper-bole, a very strong attachment between the old couple.

Barton Rivers grinned hugely, turning his insecure head into even more of a *memento mori*. 'Lovely to meet you, boys. Weather not much good for the Test Match, is it?'

This remark seemed so inapposite at the end of January, that Charles concluded the old boy must now be completely gaga. But then came a wheezing guffaw, which suggested that perhaps the comment had been a joke. Charles chuckled reassuringly.

Gerald was all politeness. Charles often felt in his friend's company that awful childish gaucheness of being with the boy whose manners one's mother has always held up as exemplary.

'I believe, sir,' the solicitor charmed, 'that we met at a Variety Artistes Benevolent Fund dinner about ten years ago.'

Barton Rivers chuckled again. 'Oh yes, must have been a Tuesday. Sun never comes out on Tuesdays.'

18

This time, surely, there was no doubt that the old boy's mind had gone. But Gerald was not so ill-mannered as to notice any inconsistency. 'Yes, I believe it was,' he went on smoothly. 'I must say, it's a great honour to meet you too, sir.'

'Honour? "What is honour? A word. What is that word, honour? Air," ' the old man quoted with sudden lucidity. Charles recognised the line of Falstaff and couldn't help thinking that soon its speaker would die, like its originator, babbling of green fields. But Barton was already off on another tangent. "Trouble is, though, the Aussies don't know the meaning of the word. All this damned bodyline bowling. You reckon there's a bump on the pitch, do you?'

Gerald replied to this direct question judiciously. 'It wouldn't surprise me at all.'

'Wouldn't surprise you at all, eh?' Barton Rivers guffawed his appreciation. 'Worthy of Noël, young man. Need new young writers with that sort of sharpness. Come and see me after the show one night, young man, and I'll introduce you to Cocky. Hear that, Dob — he said it wouldn't surprise him at all.'

'Yes, darling,' said Aurelia Howarth, and patted her husband's arm with infinite tenderness. She seemed totally unembarrassed by his disconnected chatter.

'Similar thing happened in Paris,' Barton Rivers confided to Gerald. 'No one could be sure, but I knew who was behind it.' He shook his head. 'One bad apple, you know what I mean . . .?'

Gerald nodded wisely.

Charles thought he should say something to Aurelia, to show that he hadn't noticed anything odd about her husband. Maybe something about the dog. He looked without enthusiasm at the little rat body in its shreds of silken fur, and wondered what on earth one says about, or indeed to, a Yorkshire terrier.

The answer was provided by Peter Lipscombe, who arrived at that moment with more drinks. He chucked the little dog under the chin and said, 'Hello, Cocky, everything okay?'

Cocky bit his finger.

At this moment Bernard Walton came into the bar. He was

with a neat forty-year-old man in a grey suit, and he looked worried. More than worried, he looked as if he was in shock. When Charles recognised the man in the grey suit, he thought perhaps he could guess the reason for the star's discomfiture. It was Nigel Frisch, West End Television's Director of Programmes, the man who was delaying his decision on the future of *What'll the Neighbours Say?*

Nigel Frisch threw his arms round Aurelia and thanked her flamboyantly for her performance. 'Another winner on our hands,' he effused. 'Hello, Barton.'

'Hello, old boy. Keep a straight bat, eh?' Guffaw.

'More news too, Dob darling,' Nigel continued smoothly. 'Sure you've all been in a bit of suspense over the *What'll the Neighbours . . .* situation?'

'Yes,' said Bernard Walton sharply, with uncharacteristic lack of restraint.

'As you know, it's a series that's been really successful for the audience, one that we're very grateful to you for . . .' Nigel Frisch seemed deliberately to be prolonging the agony, playing Bernard Walton along. He still spoke very casually. 'Obviously it's had its detractors. There are people that feel we've got all the mileage we can out of the situation.' He paused, sadistically. 'I don't know. Haven't really made my final decision yet. But, anyway, what I wanted to say was, we'll certainly be taking up your options for the dates proposed. So even if we don't make the series — and I dare say we will — you'll still get paid.'

Bernard Walton swayed with relief. He still looked pretty tense, but was patently glad of the news. If the company was going to commit itself to the vast outlay involved in contracting him for the next series, then they'd be bound to go ahead with it, he reasoned. 'Oh well, that's nice to hear, Nigel,' he said, recapturing some of his casualness and bonhomie. 'Let me get you a drink to celebrate.'

'I'll have a Perrier water,' said the Director of Programmes.

At that moment George Birkitt and Rod Tisdale arrived in the bar and joined the circle. Having assured Peter Lipscombe (whose finger was still bleeding slightly) that everything was okay, the former, on whom the strains of the day were beginning to tell, ordered a quadruple brandy and the latter a half of lager.

'You pleased, Rod? asked Nigel Frisch.

'All right,' the writer replied without excitement. 'Sixty-six.'

'I beg your pardon.'

'There were seventy-four jokes in the script. Sixty-six of them got laughs.'

'Ah.'

Charles slipped away from the gushing crowd. His system could only tolerate small doses of show-biz glamour. And Jane Lewis, the Trainee PA, had just come into the bar and was standing on her own.

'Can I get you a drink, Jane?'

'It's Janey.'

'Sorry.'

'Janey. With an E-Y. I decided that'd look better on the roller.'

'Roller?'

'Roller-caption. My credit at the end of the programme. Jane's so ordinary.'

'Oh. Yes. Janey then, would you like a drink?'

'Bacardi coke, please.'

Charles engaged the attention of the barman who wasn't coping with Peter Lipscombe's latest massive order, got the drinks and was encouraged to see that Jane — or rather Janey — was still alone when he returned.

She raised her glass. 'To the success of the show.'

'Hear, hear.' He took a long swallow. He was beginning to feel the effect of the day's drinking. 'How'd you think it went?'

'Part One was about 43 seconds over and Part Two was 1-17 over, but Sadie reckons they'll edit all right. And we're not certain that VTR was stable on one of the Rollback and Mixes.'

'Oh,' said Charles. 'But what about the show itself?'

She looked at him blankly. 'I've said. It was exactly two minutes over in all.'

'Yes.' He paused. 'What do you go on to after this?'

'Next I'm trailing the outside filming on the age-ist series.'

'Age-ist series?'

'Yes, W.E.T.'s just started a new unit for programmes for the elderly. Going to be presented by Ian Reynolds, who's nearly eighty. Phil Middleton — that's the director — said a lot of people would go for someone like Robert Carton as presenter, but he's too boring.'

'Ah.' Janey Lewis was clearly one of those girls who quoted irrelevant conversations verbatim. 'And after that?' Charles asked.

'Don't know. I'd like to get on to another Light Entertainment show, but I don't know. I'd like to get on to the Wragg and Bowen show.'

'Ah,' said Charles ambiguously, as if he just might know what she was talking about.

'You've heard, haven't you, that W.E.T.'s just bought Wragg and Bowen from the Beeb?'

'Of course,' Charles lied.

'Going to be a huge show, that one. I mean, Wragg and Bowen are definitely the best double act in the country. They're going to be paid ten thousand a week, each.'

'Oh. What's the show going to be like?'

'I don't think that's been worked out yet.'

'Ah.' Their conversation stagnated. Charles was feeling randy with the alcohol and didn't want to leave her. She was a remarkably attractive girl with that black hair and pale skin. Nice shape, too. If only she could talk about something other than television.

But he didn't keep his exclusive hold on her for long. Robin Laughton, the hearty Floor Manager, who appeared now to be in a lager-drinking situation, joined them. Charles found two people talking about television more than he could take, and slipped away to rejoin Gerald.

On his way across, he was accosted by another familiar figure. It was Walter Proud, who had produced Charles's previous, and ill-fated, excursion into West End Television comedy, *The New Barber and Pole Show*. He had lost more hair and there was a wildness in his eyes. 'Hello, Charles, how'd the show go?'

Charles shrugged. 'Those who know about such things seems to think it was okay.'

'Great, great. If you're going over to talk to Nigel Frisch, I'll join you.'

Something rang warning bells for Charles. 'Well, no, I

wasn't particularly . . . What are you working on here?'

'Nothing right now, actually. Got one or two projects sort of around, but, er, nothing right now.' The confession was transparent. Walter Proud was out of work.' He'd left his BBC staff job a few years before, and since then had a discontinuous sequence of short contracts with the various commercial companies. 'No, actually, I came down here to see a few chums, see if there was anything going.'

'Any luck?'

'Don't think so. I had a word with a girl who was my PA on something I did here, girl called Sadie Wainwright, but she . . . No, there doesn't seem to be much around.'

Walter's dismal tone suggested that Sadie had choked him off rather in the same way she had everyone else.

'Oh well, something'll turn up,' said Charles blandly.

'Hope so. Actually, if you are going across to see Nigel Frisch —'

But Charles was saved embarrassment by the arrival of Scott Newton. The young man looked awful. He had no colour, and his face gleamed with a fine sweat. 'Hello, Charles,' he cried, with a sad attempt at conviviality.

'Lovely performance. Can I get you a drink?'

'I think I'd better get you one. You look terrible.'

'No, I'm okay now. Had some sort of bilious bug, don't know, must have been something I ate.'

Charles caught the sour whiff of the young man's breath. He had obviously just been very sick. Something he'd eaten . . . or, more likely, just the nervous pressures of the day.

'By the way, do you know Walter Proud? You're both BBC renegades, so perhaps you've . . .'

But no, they hadn't. Charles introduced them.

'You came after the big money too, did you?' asked Walter ironically.

Scott replied in the same tone. 'Bigger, maybe, but not big enough. I seem to have even less since I made the move.'

'If that's the case, then let me buy you a drink.'

'No, no, things aren't that bad.'

They argued a bit, but Walter didn't need much convincing and Scott walked unsteadily to the bar.

'And he's directing you, Charles?' The question was

incredulous.

'Yes.'

'Good God, kids like that get jobs, while people with experience . . . If I had my way . . .'

But Charles never found out what would happen if Walter Proud had his way. The door from the fire escape into the bar suddenly burst open to admit Mort Verdon, waving his arms and screaming.

He was making so much noise that everyone was distracted and gathered round him, trying to find out the cause of his agitation.

Charles and Robin Laughton understood at the same moment that it was something he had seen outside on the fire escape, and rushed to the door. Most of the rest of the crowd followed.

It was after half-past ten and dark outside. Charles looked down the fire escape, but could see nothing untoward. The car park below was shrouded in darkness.

Then a departing member of West End Television's staff switched on the headlights of his car. A swathe of light cut across the car park.

In the middle of it, at the foot of the fire escape, lay a foreshortened figure in beige cord trousers and a flowered shirt. The light glinted on a gold necklace.

The car's headlights also played on the lower parts of the fire escape. They showed the regular parallels of painted steel and the sudden asymmetry of the railing that had given way.

The car below did not move. Its owner got out to inspect the horror he could half-see ahead.

Charles felt the press of people behind him on the small metal balcony. He looked round at the shocked faces of Robin Laughton, Bernard Walton, Rod Tisdale, George Birkitt, Walter Proud, Scott Newton, Jane Lewis and Aurelia Howarth, and at the grinning incomprehension of Barton Rivers.

There was a long silence as they all looked down at the corpse of Sadie Wainwright, and waited for someone else to be the first to say they were sorry.

Then Peter Lipscombe's cheery face appeared in the doorway. 'Hello,' he said. 'Everything okay?'

CHAPTER THREE

West End Television Ltd,
W.E.T. House,
235—9 Lisson Avenue,
London NW1 3PQ.
22nd March, 1979.

Dear Charles,

I'm sure you've already heard from your agent, but I wanted to write personally to say how delighted I am to be able to tell you that *The Strutters* is a 'go proposition'. It's really very exciting news!

I'm sorry it has taken so long for me to be in a position to pass on the news, but the 'powers that be' always take their time deliberating over this sort of thing. However, they have now made up their minds and are backing *The Strutters* all the way. Nigel Frisch really thinks it's one of the most exciting cards he holds, and reckons that with this and the new Wragg and Bowen series, W.E.T.'s going to make a very big dent in the BBC's Autumn audience figures!

Many thanks for all your hard work on the pilot, which contributed to make the show such an exciting success. I'm sure you're looking forward to the series as much as we all are — we think it's going to be very exciting! The dates will be within the option period agreed with your agent, with pre-filming probably starting the last week in May, six shows recorded on Tuesday evenings June 12th—July 17th, a couple of weeks break, and then the remaining six (which, with the pilot, will make a series of thirteen) starting on 3rd August. All sewn up by mid-September.

We at W.E.T. don't believe in changing a winning team, so the casting will all be as for the pilot, and Scott Newton, who did such a splendid job for us then, will again be directing. Rod Tisdale, whose way with a line, as you know, puts him in the Oscar Wilde class, will certainly be writing the first six scripts, though, with the pressure of time, we may bring in other writers for later episodes. But don't worry, we'll keep up the high standards we have set ourselves with that very exciting pilot!

I do hope everything is OK with you, and that you're going to be able to fit this new very exciting project into your already busy schedule. I very much look forward to seeing you for our preliminary readthrough, probably in mid-May, when we hope to assemble as many of the people who worked on the pilot as we can for the start of what I'm sure you'll agree is going to be a very exciting series.

With the warmest good wishes,

Yours sincerely,

Peter

PETER LIPSCOMBE

Producer *The Strutters*

Charles Paris had six reactions after reading the producer's letter.

1. No, he hadn't already heard from his agent, but since his agent was Maurice Skellern, possibly (and this was a bold claim, but one he believed he could substantiate) the least efficient of the breed in existence, that did not surprise him.

2. Yes, it was good news. The Inland Revenue had recently developed an unhealthy interest in his affairs and made the laughable demand that he should supply them with accounts for the last seven years. He felt betrayed by this. How did they know he had earned anything over that period? He certainly hadn't told them. He was left with the the unavoidable conclusion that the people who had actually paid him the money must have ratted on him. He reckoned it rather cheapened the magnanimous gesture of paying someone if you then went and told the tax authorities what you'd done.

3. Try as he might, he couldn't find the news as *exciting* as Peter Lipscombe evidently did. Financially encouraging, yes; good, because being in work was better than being out of work, yes; but he had great difficulty in viewing the prospect of doing fourteen lines and two moves twelve times over with anything approaching excitement.

4. If Peter Lipscombe could seriously describe what Charles had done on the pilot as 'hard work', then he

needed his head examined.

5. On the other hand, if Peter Lipscombe dared to refer to Charles's 'already busy schedule', he must be either very ignorant or capable of irony. So perhaps the 'hard work' reference was also a dig.

6. However keen the producer was to assemble everyone who had worked on the pilot, there was one person whose services he would have to forego. And that was the PA, Sadie Wainwright.

The letter made Charles think about her death again. Straight after the pilot he had thought about it quite a lot, and in the eight weeks since it had nagged occasionally at his mind.

Because of his interest in detection and the tendency, that seemed to increase with age, to find himself repeatedly involved in criminal cases, his first instinct was that Sadie Wainwright had been murdered. Falls, he reasoned, are always murders disguised. In detective fiction the next most popular question, after 'Whodunnit?', is 'Did he fall or was he pushed?'

It could have been an accident. On the evening of her death, Charles himself had noticed the rickety nature of the fire escape, and he heard later that the railing that had given way had been eaten through to nothing with rust. On the other hand, Sadie Wainwright, whatever one thought of her character, had seemed to be a supremely efficient woman. Not the sort to make silly mistakes.

Nor, from her surface behaviour, the sort to take her own life.

And, given a theory of murder, one didn't have to look far for people with a motive. Charles knew nothing of her personal circumstances, but it seemed likely that if she behaved at home anything like she did in public, she could well foment considerable resentment in a husband or lover. She had worn a chunky gold wedding ring, but that didn't mean a lot in television; Charles often thought that a broken marriage was one of the qualifications for a job in the medium.

But putting domestic fury, the most common cause of murder, to one side, the studio day had supplied an ample sufficiency of people with reasons to want her out of the way. Indeed, Charles wondered whether there was anyone working on the pilot of *The Strutters* whom she hadn't insulted.

And almost all of them could, in theory, have had the opportunity to get rid of her. He didn't know how many knew of the fire escape short cut. Presumably members of W.E.T. staff were more likely to have the information, but any one of the actors or actresses could have been told, just as he had been.

He had tried many times to reconstruct the events of that evening. He felt fairly confident that Sadie Wainwright had died after he had gone up to the bar. Though he had not actually looked down into the car park, he would surely have noticed the collapsed railing. Anyway, his natural talent for getting to bars quickly had put him ahead of most of the field of suspects.

He remembered that when he reached the bar, the only person present from *The Strutters* recording had been Peter Lipscombe, realising the full potential of his job. That seemed to rule the producer out of any conjectural list of suspects, but all the others whom Sadie had insulted remained in with a good chance. The fact that Mort Verdon, the discoverer of the body, was the only one who had appeared from the fire escape, did not mean he was the only one who had gone out there. Any murderer worth his salt would have taken the elementary precaution of returning from his crime to the bar via the more conventional lift.

Any many of the potential suspects had appeared to be in a highly emotional state. High emotion does not necessarily indicate a recent act of murder, but it can be a pointer.

Bernard Walton had looked unnaturally tense, though that could be put down to anxiety about the future of his series. Walter Proud, too, seemed to be suffering, and admitted a recent altercation with the victim of the 'accident'. And Scott Newton, the young man whose authority his PA had systematically undermined, had been a very late arrival in the bar, and had entered in a terrible nervous state. Any one of those might have had sufficient motive to kill Sadie Wainwright.

But then so might anyone else. That was what really made Charles think the death had been an accident after all. The PA had been so rude to everyone, had antagonised so many people, that it seemed invidious to attribute her death to any one individual. It was more as if the communal will had been so unanimously hostile that an indulgent God had given her a little nudge on the fire escape as a gesture of magnanimous serendipity.

Apparently, an inquest had brought in a verdict of accidental death. No doubt the police had done their customary efficient enquiries. Why should Charles Paris question their findings?

It was all a long time ago, he decided, and he needed a drink. He had been feeling very poor and made firm resolves to cut down his expenditure.

Also, as often happened when he was feeling at his most abject, he had resolved to make contact with his estranged wife, Frances.

But Peter Lipscombe's letter had shifted the mood. Though it didn't contain money, it contained the prospect of money. It gave him the confidence to risk bouncing another cheque on the way to his favourite drinking club, the tatty little Montrose round the back of the Haymarket.

And he could always ring Frances another day.

'First let me say what a pleasure it is to see you all here, and all looking so well. I get that sort of bubbly feeling that everything's going to be okay with *The Strutters*. We've got a wonderful cast, a good team, some terrific scripts, and I think the whole project's going to be jolly exciting.

'Now what I plan to do today — I'm sorry, what Scott and I plan to do today —' the producer inclined his head graciously towards his director, who acknowledged the gesture with a grin, '— is to have a leisurely readthrough of the first five scripts — Number Six will be with us soon — which wonderboy Rod Tisdale has provided for us . . .'

The wonderboy in question maintained his customary façade of a man on a bus counting the lamp-posts.

'Now this readthrough is just so's we get a feeling of the shows — we'll deal with any problems that may come up later. Since we start the filming in a couple of days, I think it's just as well that you should understand the context in which your scenes occur.'

This was a concession that didn't always happen. Charles had frequently been involved in the pre-filming of scenes

29

which were totally meaningless to him as he acted them (and often equally meaningless when he saw the completed product on the screen).

'Now we've got some really exciting locations for the series, so I think the filming should be a lot of fun.'

First time it ever has been, thought Charles sourly. His memories of filming were all of interminable waits, often in vile conditions, usually in the company of huge numbers of people with whom he had nothing in common. But he knew that directors loved it; practically every television director he'd ever met said how much he'd rather be working on film and then started the traditional moan about the demise of the British film industry. He even knew actors who enjoyed it.

'One location in particular, which we are awfully excited to have, is the one we're using for the Strutters' own house exteriors. As you know, that didn't come up in the pilot, but it was pretty well described — a large expensive house with a lot of grounds, conveniently placed on the edge of a golf course. Well, our Location Manager spent a lot of time trying to find just the right place and then — what a stroke of luck — we had the ideal house offered to us, just like that, out of the blue. And offered by someone we all know very well. Yes, good old Bernard, Bernard Walton . . . he's said we can use his place. Which just happens to fit the bill exactly . . .'

Peter Lipscombe paused for impressed reaction and got a rather apathetic murmur of appreciation. Like Charles, most of those present had come to distrust Bernard Walton's magnanimous gestures. There was usually an ulterior motive — in this case, no doubt, just to show how big-hearted he was, or to keep a kind of proprietary interest in the series, or to make sure he appeared in any publicity shots that might be taken on his premises or, thought Charles cynically, just to pocket the substantial facility fee which W.E.T. would inevitably pay for the location.

After the producer had said a few more times how exciting everything was, the readthroughs started. At first there was a certain amount of cosy laughter, but this diminished. It wasn't that the scripts got less funny — they maintained unswervingly that level of mediocrity which Peter Lipscombe had hailed as Wildean — but everyone present began to realise the sheer volume of material they had to get through. Five half-hours — even ITV half-hours which read out at twenty minutes (Rod Tisdale's work was always the right length) — was a hell of a lot of reading.

Charles got very bored as he waited for his fourteen lines per episode. However old he got, he never lost the actor's adolescent habit of counting his lines. And, though his realistic view of his status prevented him from aspiring to starring roles, it didn't stop him from finding small parts boring.

He looked around the assembly, wondering idly whether he was in the same room as the murderer of Sadie Wainwright. The little trainee, Janey Lewis, now sat in the PA's chair to the director's right, and clutched the PA's symbol of authority, a stopwatch. So she had benefited directly from Sadie's demise. Another person with a strong motive?

But then they all had strong motives. Or none of them had. Charles decided in a lazy way that he might try to find out a bit more about Sadie's background.

In the meantime, he couldn't help noticing again how attractive Janey Lewis was. She had had her hair cut shorter and more fashionably, and her clothes, too, looked newer and sharper. And there was an indefinable air of increased confidence about her. Maybe this had come with her elevation from trainee status to the full bossing rights of a real PA.

She caught his eye and smiled. Yes, she was attractive. Not mentally, really; conversation with her was like reading a manual of television technique. But physically . . . And the older Charles got, the less he thought one should dismiss the physical.

At ten to one they finished reading the third script and a folding wall of the conference room in which they sat was pulled back to reveal a lavish buffet and — yippee! — lots of bottles of wine.

Once he was armed with a plate of chicken and Scotch egg and a large glass of red wine, it wasn't difficult to buttonhole the PA. She didn't seem to mind. Charles wondered what else she might not mind. But there was a problem. Had he got the energy to mug up all the vocabulary of television — VTR and MCU and OOV and POV and all that rubbish — which would be essential in this particular seduction? He rather doubted it.

'Hello, Janey, isn't it?'

'Yes.'

'With an E-Y.' He showed off his memory.

'No.'

'What?'

'Janie with an I-E.'

'Oh, but I could have sworn you told me that . . .'

'Oh yes, I was going to have it with an E-Y, but then I noticed there's a PA at Thames who gets a credit with an E-Y, and I didn't think it looked very good on the screen — you know, a bit ordinary — so I've changed it to I-E.'

'Oh well, at least it sounds the same,' said Charles, and then, with a tiny attempt at humour, added, 'Next thing you'll be spelling it J-A-Y-N-I.'

'That's a thought,' said Janie seriously. 'I'll have to see how it looks written down.'

'Anyway, congratulations. I see you've got the Queen Bee's job now.'

'Yes, I was so lucky. You know, it was because I'd worked on the pilot, I got made up specially.'

'Made up specially?' Charles repeated, looking with mystification at her lightly freckled face which, except for a blur of green about the eyes, seemed remarkably free of cosmetics.

'Made up to PA. A lot of the girls who started as trainees with me still haven't been made up.'

'Ah.'

'Though actually Dinky's got the second PA's job on the big Wragg and Bowen show, but I reckon that's not as good as being the only PA, even if it is on a smaller show.'

'Yes, or do I mean no?'

'Anyway, Phil Middleton says he reckons sit com's the best way of learning because you do see the whole thing through, you know, with filming and studio and going right through to the VTR editing.'

Charles agreed randomly.

'The filming's going to be very exciting. Do you know who we've got as cameraman?'

'No?'

'Midge Trumper,' Janie pronounced dramatically.

'Really? Midge Trumper, eh?' said Charles, weighing the name.

'Yes. I mean, and right after *Rainbows Don't Grow On Graves.* I could hardly believe it when I heard.'

'I'm still finding it a bit difficult to take in. Midge Trumper, eh?'

'Yes.'

'Good Lord.'

Charles didn't want to spend the whole of his lunch extolling the virtues of Midge Trumper, whoever he might be, so he asked if Janie would like another drink.

'Hock-A.'

'Hock? I'm not sure. There is a dryish white. I think it's a Muscadet or —'

'No. Hock-A. Hock. . .A.'

'Hock. . .A?'

'O. . .K. Okay. It's how the Japanese say okay.'

'Oh. Okay.'

When he returned with their drinks, he managed to steer the conversation round to Janie's predecessor. 'Quite a hard act you have to follow. Though I must say the atmosphere seems a lot more relaxed without her.'

'Oh, you mean Sadie. Yes, wasn't that terrible. I mean, it's an awful way for me to get a job. I'm not complaining, but it is an awful way to get a job.'

Charles nodded and was rewarded by Janie's continuing, 'Yes, it was awful. Ernie Franklyn Junior says he reckoned anyone could've seen it coming.'

'Really?' said Charles, unwilling to break Janie's flow by asking who the hell Ernie Franklyn Junior was.

'Yes, he reckons she'd been under a lot of pressure.'

'What, at work?'

'No, no, nothing upset her at work. She could manage the job standing on her head. No . . .' She lowered her voice mysteriously. 'A man.'

'Really?'

'Yes, Ernie Franklyn Junior reckoned she'd just had a big bust-up, you know, end of some long-standing affair.'

'Oh.'

'I think it's daft to get yourself involved in that sort of thing. I believe in short flings, not getting involved.'

Charles quickly invested in the future by saying that he

fully agreed, before going on to ask if Janie had any idea who the man in Sadie Wainwright's life had been.

But no, it seemed that Ernie Franklyn Junior's information service could not supply this answer.

'But he reckons it was suicide?'

'Oh yes.'

'In spite of the findings of the inquest?'

'Oh yes. Ernie Franklyn Junior says inquests always try to avoid suicide verdicts.'

'Why?'

'Well, so that people can collect on the insurance.'

'Oh. You wouldn't happen to know who was likely to collect on Sadie's insurance?'

'No. Mind you, Ernie Franklyn Junior says —'

But the Ernie Franklyn Junior Report on the British Legal System was interrupted by the approach of Scott Newton with the Casting Director, Tilly Lake. 'Janie,' asked the director, 'could you get some copies of Script Number Five. You know, the one with the old Army friend of Colonel Strutter's in it. Tilly's got some interesting ideas on casting and wants to send some scripts out for it.'

'Yes,' Tilly Lake trilled, identifying herself (for anyone who missed the hint of the Indian silk shawl and feathered cloche hat) as an ex-actress, 'you see I'm so terribly *anti* conventional casting. I mean, especially in sit com. All directors always seem to end up using the same repertory of actors who do their job awfully well, but with no . . . depth. I mean, like this part of Colonel Strutter's army friend. I mean most sit com directors would go for someone like . . . I don't know, say, Toby Root, who's a *perfectly* good actor — lovely actor, lovely person — but I'm sure we can aim higher.'

'Ah.'

'I always try to be unpredictable. I mean, take *you*, Charles. By no means obvious sit com casting. I mean, so many casting directors, looking at the part of the golf club barman, would go for some old comedian, some actor who's famous and well-loved for a part in another sit com, but whoever booked *What'll The Neighbours* . . . said, no, let's not go for the obvious, let's think laterally and go for someone who . . . who . . .' Her sentence lost momentum.

'And they booked *you,*' she finished lamely.

'Mmm. 'Charles suppressed a grin.

But Tilly Lake was only subdued for a moment. 'So, anyway, with this part of the Colonel's friend, I think we should aim *high.* Not a Toby Root, but why not a Trevor Howard . . .'

'Just any old Trevor Howard?' asked Charles.

But she appeared not to hear him. 'Why not an . . . Olivier?'

'The simple answer is, because he'd never do it.'

'Ah, but, Charles, you don't *know* that. You never know until you ask. Perhaps he's never taken a guest role in a sit com because he's never been *asked.* I mean, we'd be able to sort out a special fee. Anyway, Scott and I think we should send him a script.'

'Certainly — what,' agreed the director gnomically.

'Incidentally, Charles . . .' Tilly Lake purred with sudden intimacy, 'your agent hasn't sent your contract back yet.'

'Ah, no.'

'I hope that doesn't mean there are any problems . . .'

'Problems? Good Lord, no. That's just the way he works.'

'Ah.'

At that moment Aurelia Howarth wafted up to the group, nursing the vile Cocky in her arms, and followed by George Birkitt. 'Scottie darling,' she cooed, 'have you any idea what time we'll be finishing today? I promised I'd ring Barton and tell him when to come round with the car.'

'Oh, Dob . . .' Tilly Lake cooed in turn. 'Don't bother Barton. The PA'll order a car for you.'

'Or I could give you a lift,' suggested Scott. 'If you don't mind the Mini. You're more or less on my way and I wanted to have a chat about —'

'No, no, Barton'll pick me up. He always does. He loves driving the Bentley. So what time, Scottie darling?'

'Let me think. I would like to have a quick word with you about something before you go, so, if we reckon to read the scripts in about . . .'

As Scott tried to estimate the shape of the afternoon, Charles sidled up to George Birkitt. 'Does she really mean that the old boy still drives?'

'Very much so.'

'God, what a terrifying thought. I'm glad I haven't got a car. I wouldn't have a moment's peace if I thought I might meet the old looney careering around in a Bentley.'

'Oh, I dare say he's safe enough. It's only his mind that's gone.'

'That's quite enough. I like to think that most people driving cars have got minds.'

'Hmm.' George seemed distracted. 'What do you think of the scripts?'

'They seem remarkably like the pilot.'

'I wonder. I think there are things that'll have to be changed,' George Birkitt said ominously. 'And I'm rather annoyed with the Wardrobe girl.'

'Really?'

'Yes. Well, as you know, I'm the last person to make a fuss about something that isn't important, but I just asked her if she could guarantee that I'd have the same dresser right through the series. It's only a small thing, but it does make a big difference. I mean, when you're concentrating on a performance, you don't want to be thinking about costume changes and things. You want to be sure that all that side is in the hands of a regular dresser you can trust. Don't you find that?'

'Oh, certainly,' agreed Charles Paris, whose eminence in his chosen profession had never merited the attentions of a personal dresser, regular or irregular.

He was pleasantly sedated with wine for the afternoon's readings, but felt a great glow of righteousness from the fact that he did not actually go to sleep. What was more, he didn't miss any of his cues. In both of the remaining scripts, he delivered his fourteen lines impeccably (impeccably, that is, in the character of Reg, the golf club barman, a character chiefly humorous for his drink problem). He felt very professional.

Round about four o'clock they finished the last script. Rod Tisdale appeared unmoved by the rendering of his *oeuvre*. Only once during the day had he spoken. That was at the end of the fourth script, when he had said, 'Peter, I think there should be a change to that line on

'Which one, Rod?'

'The Vicar's line. Where he says, "It got stuck in my cupboard." '

'Yes, got it, Rod. What should it be?'

'Can we change it to "It got stuck in my drawers"?'

'Yes, sure, Rod.'

'Silly of me, I should have thought of it earlier. Cupboard not funny, drawers funny — old rule of comedy.'

'Okay, have you all got that change?'

After all the scripts had been read, Peter Lipscombe said again that he thought it was all very exciting and Scott Newton said he thought it was all very exciting too and everyone could go, except for those who were taking part in the filming, whom Wardrobe and Make-up wanted to see. Charles Paris needed no second bidding and made off.

'Charles, Charles!' He was almost out of the building before Mort Verdon caught up with him. The tall Stage Manager had come flapping down some side stairs in pursuit and was breathless. For the readthrough he had selected a pale biscuit boiler suit and changed the diamond stud in his ear for a plain gold one.

'Charles, dear, have to give you your calls for the filming. And Wardrobe wants a word. You're a naughty boy to go off like that.'

Charles felt his hand lifted and a mock slap administered.

'But I didn't think I was in any of the filming. I thought I just stayed behind my bar.'

'No, Charles ... You must read your script, dear. At the end of Episode Four it said quite clearly "Film. Golf Club Exterior. Reg the barman chases Colonel Strutter off the premises and into his house as the captions roll." '

'So there are no words?'

'No. Just ad lib shouting.'

'Oh well, that explains why I didn't notice it. I only read the speeches.'

'Oh dear.' Mort Verdon made a *Dame aux Camelias* gesture against his forehead and then said, but not vindictively, 'I can see we're going to have trouble with *you.*'

A revolutionary thought struck Charles. 'Does this mean I'll be seen below the waist?'

'Of course.'

'But barmen are never seen below the waist. Primary rule of television.'

'First time for everything, dear. Now you come back like a good boy and have those lovely ladies in Wardrobe measure your inside leg for some trousers. I dare say you'll enjoy that.'

'These trousers'd do.'

Mort Verdon narrowed his eyes. 'That I *doubt.*'

'They were a nice pair of trousers ten years ago.'

'I was a very beautiful young man ten years ago, but it doesn't make the crows' tootsies any less prominent now.'

'I'd better come back then.'·

'Yes, boofle, that would be best.'

They were alone in the lift, so Charles hazarded a detective probe. Pity about Sadie, wasn't it?'

'Yes. Terrible.' As far as it was possible to judge through the drawl, Mort Verdon sounded as if he meant it. 'I'll miss her.'

'Really?'

'Oh yes, she was so much fun.'

'Fun!'

'Yes, dear. Wicked sense of humour.'

'That I can believe.'

'Oh yes, I know her manner was brusque and all that, but underneath she had a . . .'

He paused, gesticulating for the right word.

'You aren't going to say "heart of gold", are you?'

'Nooo,' he replied, lengthening the vowel into a long swoop. 'No, dear Sadie had a lot of qualities, but I don't think a heart of gold was among them. But she could be very funny sometimes.'

The lift stopped and they walked towards the conference room. Charles persisted with his questioning. 'Had she got a husband around?'

'No, dear, not exactly around. There had been a husband at some point, but I think she left it in South Africa when she came over here.'

'How long ago was that?'

'Don't know exactly, boofle. Must be ten years, I should think, because she was a pretty senior PA here. And of course they don't — or didn't then — have the telly in

South Africa, so she must have done all her training here.'

'Ah.' Soon they would be back with the hordes of Strutters. Charles had to be quick. 'Did Sadie have a particular boyfriend?'

'Oh, lots on and off. Most more off than on.' Mort screwed up his face in self-parody and said limply, 'Men can be bastards.' Then he dropped back to his customary level of exaggeration. 'She had just finished something that had been going on for . . . ooh, six months, I think.'

'Who was the lucky fellow?'

Mort Verdon looked at Charles with mock severity. 'Now there's no need to be ironical, boofle. I doubt if you'd know the guy, anyway. He did a series here about six months ago.'

'What was his name?'

'Walter Proud,' said Mort Verdon as he swept back into the conference room.

CHAPTER FOUR

The morning after the *Strutters* readthrough, Charles's eyes opened with their customary reluctance and closed again with their customary promptness, hoping to recapture the dwindling oblivion of sleep.

But it was no good. He was awake. After a few moments of tight-eyed pretence, he let them open again.

He supposed he should be grateful that he slept as well as he did. A lot of his contemporaries complained of long watches through the night and assumed sleeping pills to be a regular part of their diet for the rest of their days.

Charles felt a perverse righteousness from the fact that he hardly ever took sleeping pills. Such a solitary activity. His own solution to the sleep problem, alcohol, was at least taken socially. Usually. Taking sleeping pills was never social. Except in the case of a suicide pact. And that was hardly convivial.

Of course alcohol had its disadvantages, but it was so long since he hadn't woken up with a furred tongue and tender head that he hardly noticed them.

He looked round his bedsitter, trying to delay thinking

about things he didn't want to think about. The room had changed little during the seventeen years of his occupancy. He had moved into Hereford Road within a year of walking out on Frances and, except for periods of working out of town or the occasional good fortune of finding a lady willing to share her bed, he had been there ever since.

The fixtures and fittings of the room were unaltered. Still the same low upholstered chair and asymmetrical wooden one, both painted grey by some earlier occupant. The same low table, masked by magazines and papers. The fact that these now covered the portable typewriter expressed well the likelihood of Charles ever getting down to serious writing again. His own contributions to the decor, yellow candlewick on the single bed and a different plastic curtain suspended to hide the sink and gas-ring, had now been there for over ten years, and reached a kind of dull middle age that made them impossible to distinguish from the rest.

Contemplation of the room didn't cheer him.

Perhaps he should get up.

He gave this unwelcome thought a minute or two to settle in his mind.

Charles always envied people who could spring gazelle-like from bed and bound straight up the gradient of the day. He awoke always to the North Face of the mornng, and usually held long internal discussions about whether or not to call the whole expedition off, before achieving the precarious base camp of a cup of coffee, from which he could at least contemplate the arduous climb ahead.

So it was on this occasion. When he had made the coffee, he animated it with a slug of Bell's whisky. This was a practice which in principle he deplored, but increasingly he found his principles would waver in the face of life's practicalities.

With the coffee in his hand, he could delay thinking no longer.

There were two things he didn't want to think about. The first was his wife. The school of which Frances was headmistress would soon be breaking up for Easter and he really felt he should get in touch to find out whether she was going away for the holiday. In spite of their estrangement, he liked to know her movements and, though they met comparatively rarely, he could still miss her when he knew her to be away. Also, he wanted to see her.

Still, thinking of Frances did raise all kinds of emotional questions whose answers he wished to continue to evade, so he focused his mind on the less personally challenging subject of Sadie Wainwright's death.

Though he had satisfactorily accepted the common verdict of death by accident or perhaps, following the Ernie Franklyn Junior thesis, death by suicide, there was still one jarring element he couldn't reason away.

It was what he alone had heard in the Production Control cubicle on the day of *The Strutters* recording. Sadie Wainwright saying, 'You couldn't kill me. You haven't got it in you.'

If only he had heard just a few seconds more, so that he could identify who she had been addressing. The words, out of context, sounded ominous, but it was quite possible that they were just another example of show-business hyperbole.

He wished he knew a bit more about television studios and their sound systems. He knew that a variety of people could talk back into the Production Control box. Certainly the Sound and Vision Controllers on either side could. So could the four cameramen . . . and of course the Floor Managers with their little walkie-talkies. Then he was sure he'd heard PAs talking to people or places with technical names like VTR and Telecine. And there was always sound from the studio microphones on their booms.

In fact, Sadie could have been speaking from almost anywhere in the immediate studio area. That didn't give him any clues as to who she was with. Maybe it could be investigated, but two months had passed and, apart from the dauntingly technical nature of the enquiry, Charles thought it unlikely that anyone was going to remember exactly which microphone might have been left open to catch Sadie's words.

But he did now have another line of enquiry. It was one he was reluctant to pursue, because it involved a friend. But he could no longer pretend that he knew nothing of the dead girl's private life. And he had got Walter Proud's phone number.

He decided that they perhaps should meet for a drink.

Walter was very apologetic that they had to meet in a pub. 'I'd have said come round to my place, but really, I've hardly got a place for anyone to come to now.'

'Well, never mind. I'm always happy with a pub.'

But it still seemed to worry Walter. 'Thing is, I've moved from that service flat in Kensington. I'd have invited you round there, but the place I'm in now . . . well, it's really just a bedsitter.'

The emphasis he put on the last word amused Charles. 'Oh, come on, that's not the end of the world. I live in a bedsitter, you know.'

'Yes, I know. I mean, it's all right for someone like *you,* but for someone with . . .' Walter Proud realised he was on the brink of being insulting and stopped. Charles, who wouldn't have been offended anyway, wondered what the next word would have been. Standards? He certainly had standards, but on the whole they didn't concern material possessions.

Walter tried to cover up. 'What I mean is, the last few years have been a series of shocks for me. Angela and I had been married for eighteen years, you know, and we'd been in that house in Datchet for twelve. So when we split up, it was quite an upheaval. I mean, don't get me wrong — I wanted the divorce, no question, but it was . . . an upheaval. And then leaving the BBC so soon after, and I'd done . . . what? . . . fifteen years with the Corporation . . . well, it all made sense at the time, and it was the right thing to do, careerwise, but . . . er . . .'

He seemed unable to resolve the sentence.

'Do you see Angela at all now?'

'No.' Walter Proud sounded very hurt. 'No, she won't see me. I see the girls occasionally, but . . .'

'I'm sorry,' said Charles formally, giving Walter the opportunity to move on to another subject.

But the producer was unwilling to do so. 'What makes it worse is that she's ill.'

'Angela?'

'Yes. She had a growth, apparently, on her breast, about a year ago and had a . . . what do they call it . . . mastectomy. But apparently it didn't get rid of it all. It's spreading.'

'Oh.'

'I only hear this from the girls, you know. I keep offering

to go and see Angela, but they say, no, she doesn't want to see me and . . . I don't know, it makes me feel terrible.'

'Let me get you another drink.' Charles tried another way of breaking the flow, but when he returned with a large gin and tonic and a pint of bitter for himself (still irrigating the brain, move back on to the scotch later), Walter continued.

'You break up a marriage because it doesn't work and because you want to get around a bit, see a few more other women, have a bit of *life* for God's sake, before you're too old, and then you come up against something like this. And you realise perhaps you are too old, that you're now in the generation to whom illnesses happen, and you should have just stuck together, because there really isn't any time.'

Charles felt a cold pang of depression. Walter's situation was too close to his own for comfort. Suppose something happened to Frances. Suppose she became ill or, worse, was suddenly killed in an accident, and he was nowhere around . . . He must ring her.

Walter's tale of woe wasn't making it easy for him to get round to the real purpose of their meeting. It was bad enough suspecting a friend of murder, but to interrogate a friend in this sort of state was really kicking a man when he was down.

Fortunately, Walter seemed to realise how low he was getting and made a determined effort to pick himself out of his slough of despond. With something approaching the old bravado Charles remembered, he said, 'Still, a man has to do what a man has to do. I don't really regret any of it. Okay, I was very cosy at the BBC, and, to some extent, at home, but I was dying on my feet. At least I've seen a bit more of life and things by cutting loose.'

'Things . . . being women?' Charles fed gently.

Walter responded to this man-of-the-world approach. 'Oh yes, there have been one or two. It's only when you're on your own that you realise quite how many of them there are.'

Charles laughed conspiratorially, hoping to stimulate further information, but got nothing more than an answering chuckle. He would have to be a bit more direct in his approach. 'Down at W.E.T. the other day someone was saying you'd had a bit of a fling with someone there.'

'Oh yes.' Walter smiled a Lothario smile, but then seemed to recollect something unpleasant and changed his manner. 'Yes, it was very unfortunate. The girl died.'

'Really?' said Charles ingenuously.

'Yes, she was . . . well, you were there.'

'I was there?'

'When you were making that pilot, you remember, the girl who fell off the fire escape.'

'Oh, Good Lord, you mean that PA? What was her name . . . Sadie?'

'Sadie Wainwright.' Walter nodded. 'Yes, we had a thing. It went on . . . well, on and off . . . for two or three months.'

'How awful for you, for her to have . . .'

'Yes, it was pretty upsetting. But in fact the affair was over, had been for a month. Didn't work.'

'But I seem to remember . . .' (Charles tried to disguise the interrogation in casualness) '. . . that you said you'd talked to her on that evening.'

'Oh, talked to her, yes. We were still on speaking terms . . . at least I'd thought we were . . .'

'You mean she wasn't pleased to see you?'

'She was bloody rude, if you must know.'

'Seems to have been a habit with her.'

'Yes, she had a sharp tongue. Mind you, that was only her manner. She could be very . . . well, different.' Walter Proud seemed to recollect some moment of tenderness, but quickly snapped out of the mood. 'No, I'd gone to see her because she knew everything that was going on at W.E.T. I thought she might know of something coming up for me. The fact is, Charles, not to put too fine a point on it, I am out of a job. I've been out of a job now for five months. I've tried writing round all the companies, going to see people, using every contact I've ever made, and all of them lead to the same answer — nothing doing.'

'Couldn't you go back to the Beeb?'

'No chance. They're in as bad a state as anyone else. Worse. They've got no money and can't think of taking on new staff. And if they did, I don't think people who resigned three years ago at the age of fifty-four would be top of the list. The BBC is very paternalistic and looks after you very well, so long as you remain on the staff. But if you commit the unforgivable affront of resigning, well, you look after yourself, matey. It's fair enough, but I'm afraid it means, in answer to your question, No, under no circumstances could I go back to the Beeb.'

'Something'll come up,' Charles offered meaninglessly.

'It'd better. Needless to say, I've screwed up the full pension I would have got if I'd stayed.'

'Have you got any savings?'

Walter laughed shortly. 'Never had any. By the time I'd sorted out the divorce and moved a couple of times ... And then being out of work is bloody expensive. Trying to get jobs is, anyway. I mean, if you're chatting up an old friend who happens to be a Programme Controller some-where, then you take him out to the sort of lunch you would have taken him out to in the old days. Except of course in the old days, you would have had an expense account. When you're paying with real money, boy, you notice the difference.'

'So Sadie ...' Charles steered the conversation back on to the course he required.

'Yes, Sadie was a last-ditch attempt. A contact. I thought she might know the scene at W.E.T. Tell me if they'd got all the producer/directors they needed for the new stuff they were doing. I mean, I know they've got Wragg and Bowen coming up, and I worked with them at the BBC. And then there's this series for the elderly. A real F.G., if ever I heard one.'

'F.G.?'

'Franchise-Grabber. You may have been aware, Charles, that all the ITV companies' franchises run out in a year or so. And so suddenly all of them have started doing very worthy programmes — stuff for minorities, heavily sub-sidised operas, all kinds of noble enterprises that they wouldn't normally do in a million years. It's just so that they can show the IBA what public-spirited and responsible companies they are, and why they ought to continue to have their franchises and continue to make huge amounts of money from their usual run of crap.'

This cynicism was unlike Walter, who had always been one of those people, like Peter Lipscombe, who found television enormously *exciting*. He read Charles's reaction.

'Well, I'm just sick of the whole bloody business. God, I wish I'd just stayed in the BBC and coasted quietly down to my pension. Even taken an early retirement. I don't think I'd have any pride left about that sort of thing now. Have you any idea what it's like going round to people all the time, *begging* them to employ you?'

Charles shrugged. 'I'm an actor.'

'Yes, of course, so you know all about it. But at least you've had practice. I find it's a bit late in life for me to learn how to cope with it.'

'But Sadie,'Charles insisted mildly, 'couldn't help?'

'Wouldn't help certainly. Probably couldn't either.' He looked very doleful. 'Oh, she was probably right.'

'What did she say?'

'That I was past it. Past everything, she said. Certainly washed up as a television producer.'

'Oh, come on. You did some terrific stuff in the past.'

'In the past, yes. And what have I got to show for it? A few press clippings, some stills, cassettes of the later stuff — though that's ironical; I can't afford to keep up the rental of my video cassette recorder, so that's gone back. So I've got nothing. Not even Angela. She's dying quietly in Datchet and here am I drinking gin I can't afford and . . .'

Walter Proud seemed to be on the verge of tears, which Charles didn't think he could cope with. He wrenched the conversation brutally on to another tack. 'That evening of the pilot, when you came to see Sadie, when did you arrive?'

'When did I arrive?' the producer repeated blankly.

'Yes.'

Suddenly Walter started to laugh. It was a weak and not a jovial sound. 'Oh, Charles, I don't believe it.'

'What?'

'You're off on one of your bloody detective trips, aren't you?'

'Well . . .'

'Now you think Sadie was murdered and —'

'I think there may have been something strange about the death. I mean, she was a grown woman, she hadn't been drinking, why should she suddenly fall off the fire escape.'

46

The railing gave way.'

'Or was helped to give way . . .'

'Oh really.'

'I'm not the only person who said that.'

'What, you mean all those self-dramatising fools at West End Television think someone gave her a shove?'

'Not that, necessarily. She might have done it herself.'

'Suicide?'

'Possible.'

'Not if you knew Sadie.' Realisation dawned on Walter. 'You mean, you thought she might have . . . because of me? Because we'd broken up, you thought she might . . . oh, Charles. It's so wrong it's almost flattering. No, I'm afraid I didn't rate that highly on her list of priorities. I was a few bouts of sex before she decided I was . . . what was her expression . . . past it? I don't think I was bloody past it, I think anyone would have found the same with her. I really think she was a nymphomaniac. I don't mean the kind of avid partner one dreams of, but the real thing, someone with a pathological and insatiable desire for sex. It's not very pleasant when you encounter it.'

Charles, who never had, agreed uncertainly. And, since any cover he might have had had been thoroughly blown, asked, 'And you didn't kill her?'

'No, no, sorry. There were times when it might not have been a bad idea, but I'm afraid I never thought of it.'

'So what time did you arrive at W.E.T. that evening?'

'Oh, I see, the full interrogation. I don't get off the hook so easily. Right, I got there about nine. I have cause to remember that, because the doorman wouldn't let me in. Good God, I've produced two or three series for the company, and he wouldn't let me in to the building. Said I had to be vouched for by a member of staff. I got him to page practically every name I could remember ever having met there before I found someone who'd vouch for me and let me in to get a drink. That's the sort of thing that destroys you, Charles. You don't think about it when you've got a job, but, God, it tears you up when you find yourself crawling to doormen like some unwanted alien.'

Charles felt relief. He hadn't wanted to suspect his friend, but he had had to check it. If Walter really had arrived at nine in the evening, and that could be confirmed, then he could not possibly have been the person whose death threat Sadie Wainwright had treated with such contempt. And since those few overheard words were the only real reason why Charles had any suspicions about the accident, Walter seemed effectively to have left the list of suspects.

'So you saw Sadie after the pilot recording finished at ten?'

'That's right. I met someone in the bar who told me what she was doing that evening and waylaid her as she came out of the studio. I suggested a drink and got my head bitten off, so I said what I really wanted to ask her and . . .'

'Had your other head bitten off?'

'Exactly.'

'So you didn't see her for long?'

'No, she was very short with me. Said she had other fish to fry. And from the tone of her voice I could have believed she meant it literally. I knew the signs well enough to recognise them. She was spoiling for a row with someone.'

'You don't know who?'

'I know where. She didn't even stop to talk to me. I had to tag along by her side while she marched ahead to sort out the next poor sod. She just marched into his dressing room and I heard her say before the door closed, "Right, what is all this, you bastard?" '

'Who was in the dressing room?'

'Ah, I don't know.'

'Which number was it?'

'Number Three.'

Number Three, the dressing room whose allocation to him had caused such affront to Bernard Walton.

CHAPTER FIVE

Filming days always start uncomfortably early. Charles had had a make-up call at seven o'clock. A car had been sent to fetch him, which he might have thought was a flattering recognition of his raised status as an actor if he hadn't seen the prodigality with which television companies send out cars to deliver scripts, pick up cassettes or collect take-away meals. Needless to say, at six-thirty in the morning the driver's tattoo on the front door at Hereford Road had failed to wake Charles, but had disturbed the hive of lumpish Swedish girls who occupied the other bedsitters. With their sing-song remonstrances and the driver's belligerent complaints at being kept waiting, he had left the house in some confusion.

But as he was made up, he relaxed. He always found it a pleasant experience. In the theatre he was used to doing it himself, and to have someone doing it for him was a great luxury. Besides, make-up girls are by tradition extraordinarily attractive. And to sit half-asleep in a comfortable chair while a sweet-smelling girl caresses your face must be the definition of one sort of minor bliss.

Its only disadvantage is that, like all blisses, it is too short. Only seconds after he had sat down, it seemed, the gentle facial massage stopped, a discreet tap on the shoulder made him open his eyes, he had another second to gaze deeply into the brown eyes of the make-up girl, and then it was time to go and join the rest of the cast in the coach which would take them to the location. *Sic transit gloria mundi.* (So it is that transport brings us from the glorious to the mundane.)

On the coach, Charles saw that George Birkitt had an empty seat beside him and made towards it, but the actor indicated a pile of scripts and said, 'Sorry, old boy, lot of studying to do. I seem to have a damned lot of lines to learn for this bloody filming.'

So Charles went and sat by Debbi Hartley, the actress who played the Strutters' *au pair*. She was a pretty little blonde of about twenty-five, but he had never fancied her. She was the clone of too many other pretty little actresses of twenty-five, and her self-absorption was so great that it was almost impossible to think of her in a sexual context.

She did not seem to object to his company, and started animatedly into a monologue about the wisdom of having her hair cut short once the *Strutters* series was over. Whereas her agent thought it would make her look younger, certain of her friends were of the opinion that it might make her look older. This was obviously of enormous relevance because when one went up for an interview

(Charles had noticed how the new generation of actors never used the word 'audition'), first impressions were vital and if the director thought of one as too old, one wouldn't stand a chance for ingenue roles, or if he thought of one as too young, then one wouldn't get the sort of *femme fatale* parts, because no one ever realised how versatile one was and it was so difficult to avoid getting typecast, but she, Debbi, thought she was just at the stage in her career to do something a bit different, so showing she could do other things as well as the little-bit-of-fluff parts, what did Charles think?

Since he didn't really think anything, he didn't say anything, but his lack of response did not deflect Debbi from the course of her debate.

Charles looked round. The coach was filling up. Mort Verdon stood at the front, checking names against a clipboard. Janie Lewis entered importantly, carrying piles of bits of paper. He contemplated joining her and exchanging discussion of hair length for that of the relative merits of film and mobile VTR recording, quoted directly from Ernie Franklyn Junior or some other guru of the W.E.T. canteen. There wasn't much to choose in conversation; the only difference was that he did fancy Janie, whereas he didn't fancy Debbi.

On the other hand ... By the time the coach was on Westway, his eyes had closed. Beside him, Debbi Hartley continued to enumerate her virtues as an actress. It was half an hour before she noticed he was asleep.

Bernard Walton lived in a large house, set on a hill between Cookham and Bourne End. Charles woke up as the coach turned off the main road into his drive. The house was at this point invisible because of the steepness of the incline, but the approach was impressive. A gravel drive zigzagged up through immaculately planted gardens. Neat stone walls bordered it and on these, at intervals, stood tall terracotta urns from which variegated displays of flowers spilled.

As the coach groaned and protested through its lowest gears on the hairpin turns, its occupants could see the view the house commanded. At the foot of the hill, green, flat water-meadows spread to the broad gleam of the Thames. Beyond, woods obscured most signs of human habitation.

Round one last corner and they saw the house itself. It was Thirties Tudor, black and white, not scoring many aesthetic marks, but impressive just for its bulk and position. A tennis court and a service cottage brought right angles to the landscaped curves of the garden. Beyond a neat privet hedge could be seen the polite undulations of a golf course. If the whole location had a manufacturered air, it was very fitting for the character of its owner.

Bernard Walton stood in front of the large oak door waving welcome. More than welcome, he was waving possession and condescension. By allowing *The Strutters* to use his home, he had given the series his seal of approval. But he had also diminished it, as if it existed only by his mandate.

Charles caught George Birkitt's eye. 'Ostentatious bugger,' murmured the star of *The Strutters*.

'All part of the image,' said Charles lightly.

'Yes. God, if I had his money, I hope I'd show a little bit more reticence.' But there was a note of wistfulness in George Birkitt's voice. Bernard Walton's house had struck a psychological blow against him. He might be the star of *The Strutters* and he might be about to make a great deal of money. But he hadn't made it yet. Whatever his fancies, he had still a long way to go to catch up with a real, established star.

Bernard Walton greeted them effusively. 'Do make yourselves at home. I'm just pottering around today, so ask if there's anything you need. The *Sun's* coming down to do an interview this morning and I'm recording a few links for some radio show this afternoon, but otherwise I'm completely at your disposal. Do remember you're my guests.'

This was pure Bernard Walton and Charles couldn't help admiring it. He felt sure the star had deliberately set up the newspaper and radio bits to coincide with the filming day, so that no one should forget his importance. The pose of the self-denying host was also typical, and it was a gesture that was very easy to make. The usual filming back-up services, location caterers, make-up caravans and so on, already had their transport drawn up on the gravel. Even lavatories were available in the various vehicles, so the demands on Bernard Walton's hospitality would be minimal. And he would certainly have arranged a suitable fee with the Location Manager to cover any mild disruption which the filming might occasion.

Already there were a few signs of activity around the location. Men in blue nylon anoraks moved cables and huge lights on wheeled tripods. Make-up girls checked for any deterioration in their handiwork that the coach trip might have caused. Dressers inspected their costumes for invisible flecks. Mort Verdon flounced around checking props. The men whose only function seemed to be to wear lumberjack checked shirts wore their lumberjack checked shirts and discussed overtime rates ominously. Midge Trumper (yes *the* Midge Trumper), the cameraman, inspected his camera. Janie Lewis, her neck festooned like a Hawaiian princess's with pens on thongs and stopwatches on thongs, moved about, aimlessly purposeful.

But there seemed no momentum to any of the activity. It wasn't just the slow pace of everything, which is *de rigueur* in television, there was an even greater lack of purpose. It took Charles a minute or two to realise that this was due to the absence of the director.

Scott Newton had not been in the coach; he had insisted on coming to the location under his own steam.

Even as Charles remembered this, the throaty roar of an engine and a fusillade of gravel announced Scott Newton's arrival and the nature of the steam under which he was arriving.

A brand-new silver Porsche screeched to a halt beside the coach and the young television director bounced out, looking, in his tinted glasses, his ginger corduroy blouson suit and his white soft-leather French boots, exactly as a young television director should look.

'Morning, crew and artists,' he cried. 'Let's get this show on the road. Is everyone here?'

Mort Verdon fussed up to him. 'Not quite everyone, dear. Dob wasn't coming in the coach. Hasn't arrived yet.'

'Okay, let's start with one of the other set-ups that doesn't involve her. What about the Colonel being chased by Reg the barman?'

Slowly this message filtered through, and men and equipment started to move slowly to the side of the house where the first set-up was to be. Even the men whose only function was to wear lumberjack checked shirts deigned to wear them over there.

Charles couldn't help noticing the new confidence that illuminated Scott Newton. He decided that it was because they were filming. Film still has a glamour and tradition, and it is easier for a director to fit into the supercool Hollywood stereotype on location than it is in the prosaic and crowded setting of a studio. But Scott Newton was also obviously in the money. The new clothes and, more than that, the new car made it clear that his agent had negotiated a very favourable contract for *The Strutters*. Scott Newton no longer looked like a man with financial worries.

Charles found himself beside the young man while they waited for George Birkitt to change into the relevant tweeds for the scene ahead and, because he thought Scott would appreciate it, commented that the Porsche was a very smart motor.

Scott's reaction proved him right. Clearly not enough people had made the observation. 'Yes, not bad, is it?' he agreed airily. 'Really good to feel a bit of power under your foot. Drinks petrol, of course, but . . .' he shrugged, '. . . if you want the power . . .'

'Must have set you back a bit.'

'It's leased, actually. Makes sense. My accountant says I'm going to have to pay so much in tax this year that I may as well offset what I can.'

Yes, his agent had certainly negotiated a good contract. Life seemed to have come right for Scott Newton. Any agonising he might have had about the wisdom of leaving the BBC had dissipated. He was now director of a major series, which would lead to other major series and . . . Nothing could stop him.

Charles couldn't help thinking of Walter Proud. He had once talked in exactly the same brashly confident tones.

A further scrunching of gravel and the sound of an altogether more sedate, but no less powerful engine than the Porsche's, now interrupted the proceedings and announced the arrival of Aurelia Howarth and Barton Rivers.

The vintage Bentley was a green monster with its hood

53

fixed back in honour of the warm weather. The couple behind the windscreen looked like its first owners. Aurelia wore a large hat bound round with a silk scarf, and Barton Rivers had added a white flat cap and white gloves to his uniform blazer. When he tottered, spidery, from the car and went round to open his wife's door, he revealed again white flannels and black shoes.

The arrival, like that of visiting royalty, suspended all other activity and everyone drifted over towards the car. Scott Newton got there first, still full of his new possession. 'What do you think of the car, Dob?'

'Very nice, dear.'

As with Charles, he couldn't resist boasting of his affluence. 'Expensive to run, mind . . .'

'I'm sure you'll manage, dear.'

'I'm sure I will, Dob.'

At that moment Bernard Walton, who was going to miss no opportunity of asserting his authority over the day, once again materialised from the house and, throwing his arms around Aurelia, gushed, 'Dob darling, lovely to welcome you here again. Always such a pleasure to see you, whether the call is purely social or, as today, when you're working. Hello, Barton, old boy.'

Barton Rivers did his death's head grimace. 'Nice to see you, dear boy. Lovely day for the match, what?'

Mort Verdon busied up to the leading lady. 'Aurelia boofle, sorry to interrupt, but I have to chivvy you, dear. Time to get into your cossy and have your slap done.'

'Yes, of course, darling. Must just see to Cocky. The little darling's in his little basket in the back of the car, and he does so hate his little basket.'

'Of course,' sympathised Mort, whose pressure was always discreet, and who knew that Aurelia wouldn't settle until she had settled the dog. He followed her to the car, in case she needed any help with her darling.

George Birkitt, standing beside Charles, was less sympathetic. 'Bloody dog. I thought she'd have left it behind. This whole bloody production seems to revolve round that pooch.'

'Doesn't do much harm,' said Charles mildly.

'Huh. It offends me. I wonder if they make mousetraps big enough,' George Birkitt mused.

Charles chuckled, but when he looked at his fellow-actor, there was no smile on the other's face.

Cocky was released from his wicker prison and celebrated his freedom by leaping around everyone's legs, yapping. 'How is the little love?' asked Bernard Walton with a great deal of warmth, though, shrewdly, he kept his distance.

'Ah, he's not a very well boy. The nasty old vet says he's not a well boy.'

'Good,' murmured George Birkitt. 'That's the best news I've heard all week.'

'Come on, boofle,' urged Mort Verdon tactfully. 'I think we'd better get changed for the filming.'

'Of course, darling. Now where are the dressing rooms?'

'It's just caravans, I'm afraid, dear.'

'Oh.'

She spoke the word coolly, without real disapproval, but Bernard Walton saw another opportunity to demonstrate his magnanimity. 'Dob darling, come and change in the house. Honestly, I hate to think of you cramped in some awful caravan, while the house is just here. Come on, love, you can go into the guest room where you stayed last time you were down. Barton, you come along, old boy.'

And, before anyone could remonstrate, Bernard Walton led the royal pair into the house, with a rabble of commoners, dressers and make-up girls trailing behind.

'Make you bloody sick,' said George Birkitt savagely. 'Turning up bloody late, disrupting everything, no apologies. I just don't think it's professional.'

Charles shrugged. 'I think it's remarkable she gets here at all, at her age. Particularly with dear old Barton Rivers driving.'

But George Birkitt was not mollified. 'What I object to is the fact that I got up at six to get to W.E.T. for my make-up call, came in that bloody coach with everyone else, and she has the nerve to just roll up about ten o'clock, and of course she isn't in make-up, so everything's behind. And no one ticks her off or anything, everything just bloody stops and we all bow and scrape and grin inanely for a quarter of an hour until her ladyship allows us to get on with our work. I mean, you know I'm the last person to make a fuss, but I do think somebody ought to say something. Peter, or Scott. God, how I hate all this *star* business.'

'Oh, come on. She's an old lady. Deserves a few allowances.'

But George Birkitt wasn't listening. 'I think, for the next day's filming, I'll drive myself down.'

The filming started, and made its usual, infinitesimally slow progress. Once again Charles realised why film stars were paid so much. If they could stand the constant repetition, the constant disruption, the tiny daily advance, then they earned every dipenny. For him, working in film had all the appeal of building a ten-foot model of the World Trade Centre out of matchsticks.

He was fortunate, or not, according to how you looked at it, to get his scenes out of the way early on. Under Scott Newton's perfectionist direction, they only spent about an hour and a half on Reg the barman chasing Colonel Strutter the twenty yards from the privet hedge to the house. Another day, in another location, they would have to film the beginning of the chase, the segment from the golf clubhouse to the privet hedge. (Because the clubhouse adjacent to Bernard's house was in the wrong style for the decor of the studio set already built, they were doing that sequence at a different club.)

Charles was told that an hour and a half for thirty seconds of film without written dialogue was not bad going, though to him it seemed very slow. It meant that by twelve o'clock he had discharged his obligations for the day, and was in theory free to leave. On the other hand, he was a long way from a station, and no one seemed likely to be driving anywhere until the day's filming was over. So he might as well stay around until the coach returned.

He didn't really mind. He had noticed that there were some crates of wine in the location caterers' minibus. He felt relatively content.

The only thing that made him feel less than completely content were the trousers that Wardrobe had reckoned to be right for Reg the barman. Charles liked trousers better the longer he wore them. His two main pairs had a combined age of twenty-one years and now he never noticed that he had them on. The ones Wardrobe had chosen for the rare, probably never-to-be-repeated appearance of a barman's bottom half, felt stiff, tickly and alien.

At twelve-thirty sharp they all broke for lunch. (The Union rules were no less closely observed because they were on location. Indeed, over the few days Charles had been involved with *The Strutters* series, he had noticed an even greater consciousness of Union rules. Maybe this was another symptom of the approaching industrial trouble which George Birkitt had forecast at the time of the pilot.) Bernard Walton was in no way inconvenienced by the arrangements, though it appeared that he had swept Aurelia Howarth and Barton Rivers off for a private lunch in the house. The location caterers opened up their double-decker bus to reveal rows of tables and chairs, and served a substantial meal of truffled pork pâté, cold duck with a wide variety of salads, and fresh strawberries (not cheaply available in May), washed down with a choice of, or, if you felt like it, a mixture of, red and white wines.

Since he hadn't been involved in the recent filming, Charles was early in the queue and sat down alone with his loaded plate and a large glass of red wine. Two of the men whose only function was to wear lumberjack checked shirts, and therefore hadn't been involved in the filming at all, sat down opposite and, oblivious, proceeded to discuss their profession.

'You reckon he'll overrun?' asked the older one.

'Don't know. He seems to be more or less up to schedule.'

The other one grimaced. 'Might pass the word round to the lads to cool it a bit, or we won't get into the overtime.'

'Yeah.'

'Incidentally, I need a fiver off of you.'

'What for?'

'Oh, do own up. You come in my car with Rog and Bill, we're all going to claim the first-class rail and taxi link, I got to get a cut for depreciation on my motor.'

'Have Rog and Bill paid up?'

'Sure'

'Okay then. There you are.'

'You on this filming for the Wragg and Bowen thing next week?'

'Yeah.'

'Reckon we're on to a flier there.'

'What, you mean we'll have to stay overnight?'

'No, no, sonny. The location's only an hour and a half down the motorway. No, we only *claim* the overnights, don't *do* them.'

'Sure.' A pause over the truffled pâté. 'You reckon it's all all right today?'

'Filming? Yeah, okay, I reckon. Mind you, I'm just waiting for him to do a shot that's got one of the greens of the golf course in it.'

'Why's that?'

'Haven't you noticed, son? They've got the sprinklers on.'

'So?'

'Oh, come on, where was you brought up? If you got running water in the shot, then you got to have a plumber on the set, haven't you. Specialist work, son. Need a fully paid-up plumber when you're using sprinklers.'

'Didn't know that.'

'You got a lot to learn, son. Have a word with Rog, he'll fill you in about your rights.'

'I must do that. Oh well, cheers.'

They raised their glasses and drank. The older one grimaced at the taste. ''Ere, I don't reckon this lot's château-bottled. Might have a word to Rog about that, and all.'

The arrival of George Birkitt beside him prevented Charles from concentrating further on this illuminating conversation. Colonel Strutter's mood had not improved.

'Did you see that? Bloody Bernard Walton's taken bloody Aurelia and her lunatic husband off to lunch.'

'They've known each other a long time.'

'Huh. Well, I don't think there should be any discrimination of that sort. We're all of us actors, for God's sake, neither more nor less.' He took a mouthful of pâté. 'And notice I wasn't invited to the private lunchipoos.'

'Don't worry, the food's not bad here.' He reached out to fill his glass a third time from the bottle of red wine.

'Not too much of that, Charles. Got to work this afternoon.'

'You have, George. I haven't. I'm finished.'

'Oh yes. Well, Charles, do watch it in future. I've got a lot of scenes with you in this series, and I've got enough to do without worrying whether you're going to be sober enough to remember the lines.'

'I'll be very careful,' said Charles, mock humility masking his annoyance.

'Good.'

'Mind you, though, George, I am one of those actors who has always been said to be B.W.P.'

'B.W.P.?'

'Better when pissed.'

The location caterers had no sense of economy. W.E.T. was paying, so they didn't mind the half-finished plates left by technicians who had overestimated their capacity. They seemed content to scrape half-full terrines into their rubbish bins. And they had no objection at all to Charles Paris appropriating a bottle of red wine to see him through the afternoon. (In fact, when he offered to pay them for it, they looked at him as if he were the first of some newly hatched species hitherto unseen on this planet.)

So, since it was a nice sunny day, and since Bernard Walton's garden was a very pleasant place to loll in, Charles spent a pleasant afternoon lolling. Occasionally he would stroll back to the filming to show a token interest, but nothing ever seemed to be happening. They were always waiting. Waiting for the sun to emerge from behind a cloud. Waiting for an aeroplane to pass, so that its sound wouldn't affect the recording. Waiting, on one occasion as Charles passed, for Debbi Hartley to complete a costume change.

This had clearly been taking some time. The men whose function it was to wear lumberjack checked shirts were looking at their watches and smiling, as the odds on over-time shortened. Scott Newton and Peter Lipscombe, who had appeared at some point during the day to see that everything was okay, were looking extremely frustrated. At last the director could contain himself no longer. 'Oh, for Christ's sake!' he cried. 'What the hell is she changing into?'

'An actress?' Mort Verdon asked, almost inaudibly.

59

Once, just for a change of scene, Charles wandered down the steep zigzag of the drive towards the main road. He had it vaguely in his mind to walk along by the river. An interest in fishing, which he had not recently indulged, drew him to rivers. But when he got to the bottom, he saw that the Thames was a good deal further away than it had looked. There was a two-mile stretch of fields to traverse, so he turned round and started back up the drive.

It really was steep. It made him realise, gloomily, just how out of condition he was. Not enough exercise, too much booze. He knew he should take more of the first and less of the second, but something stubborn within him resisted the notion. It made him think of Frances. That was the sort of advice Frances would give him. She was nearly always right. That was what at times annoyed him about her and made him, perversely, turn against her advice.

He must ring her, though.

Half-way up the drive he felt puffed and sat on the wall for a moment by one of the tall flower-filled urns. He leant his back against it, but it wobbled, so he sat upright and looked over the deep green to the Thames.

Must start fishing again, he thought. Must start fishing, and must see Frances. In some way, the two intentions seemed related. Could it be that both of them offered the prospect of a kind of peace?

The day's filming finished in time. At twenty past five, Scott Newton said the magic words, 'It's a wrap,' and it was all over. The director looked buoyantly confident. The men in lumberjack checked shirts looked disgruntled for a moment, and then started dismantling everything with a speed and efficiency that hadn't been approached during the day. There were fixed payments for their tidying-up time, so there was no point in hanging about.

Everyone was now in a hurry to be off. The actors made for the coach. They still had ahead of them the tedious business of returning to the W.E.T. dressing rooms where their day clothes were. Aurelia Howarth, to the annoyance of Wardrobe, said that she and Cocky were tired and so she'd go home in her frock and bring it back the next day. Barton Rivers appeared, white-gloved and grinning, to squire her to the Bentley. He shook everyone's hands and urged everyone ghoulishly to play up, play up, and play the game.

The traffic jam on the gravel in front of the house was increased when Bernard Walton brought his dark blue Rolls-Royce Silver Cloud out of the garage. He had to be up in Town for the Charity First Night of some new movie, and was suddenly dressed in a midnight-blue dinner suit, with a midnight-blue butterfly bow at the neck of a froth of pale blue shirt. He didn't lock the house, since his housekeeper remained. (Bernard Walton was unmarried. He and his Publicity Manager had not yet found a woman who would keep her fashion value long enough for him to justify this step.)

Charles, in the mellowness of the afternoon's wine, felt confident that however the traffic was sorted out, the coach would probably be the last to leave, so he didn't rush into it to sit and wait.

The Bentley went first, its huge power held back to cope with the dangerous curves of the hill. Aurelia turned and waved, while Barton grinned ahead. They looked like something out of a Thirties film. The noise of the engine faded quickly to silence as they passed out of sight. The steep bank cut off sound quickly and ensured that the domestic calm of the great Bernard Walton should not be disturbed by the vulgar sounds of traffic on the main road below.

Bernard himself set off next, the Rolls moving faster than the Bentley, secure in its knowledge of every contour of the steep drive. Once again the powerful engine sound died quickly.

Scott Newton moved over to the side of his Porsche, his face beaming the unrestrainable smile of a father with his first daughter. But once there he hesitated. He wanted to make a departure which would be noticed, or rather by which his car would be noticed, but he wasn't sure how to time it.

The sight of Peter Lipscombe came to his rescue. The producer, having checked with everyone that everything was okay, was about to get into his company BMW and return to London. Scott Newton called across to him, 'Last one back to W.E.T.'s a sissy.'

The producer smiled. 'I'll be back before you, Scott.'

'No chance. Yours doesn't go as fast as this.'

'I'm not saying it does. But I know the back ways when we get to Town. You may get there first, but I'll beat you through the rush hour. I've done it back from here within the hour.'

'Want a bet on it?'

'Fiver.'

'You're on.'

The producer and director walked towards each other and shook hands. 'What's more,' said Peter Lipscombe, 'I'm so confident I'll beat you, that I'll let you go first.'

Scott Newton thought for a second, but then decided to take advantage of the offer and make his exit while everyone was still watching. He leapt into the silver Porsche, gunned the engine and shot off in a burst of gravel.

The sound of the engine faded, but just before it disappeared, the note changed to a scream of metal. This was followed by a series of heavy thuds, and then a great boom which seemed to shake the hill on which the house stood.

Charles Paris reached a viewpoint of the accident a little behind the younger men who had rushed down the drive. There was no doubt what had happened.

Round one of the hairpins in the drive, an urn lay in the middle of the gravel, its bright confusion of flowers spilled in the fall. The ridges swept up by the Porsche's tyres showed how Scott, coming on the obstruction blind and too fast, had swerved to avoid it. And how the car had got out of control.

The scarred flower beds and uprooted shrubs charted its passage down the hill. The jack-knifed TIR lorry from Spain showed what it had met when it reached the main road.

And, because there was nothing else in sight that could be it, the shapeless mass like crumpled kitchen foil must have been the silver Porsche.

CHAPTER SIX

West End Television Ltd,
W.E.T. House,
235—9 Lisson Avenue,
London NW1 3PQ.
30th May, 1979.

Dear Charles,

Just a note to fill you in on developments on *The Strutters* front. Obviously we were all very shocked by what happened but we mustn't let our imaginations run away with us. People are talking about our two misfortunes and saying they must be connected and that it's a bad luck show and . . . All rubbish! The show must go on and the show will go on. There is no danger of anything stopping the advance of this very exciting project.

I am delighted to be able to tell you that we now have a new director for the series, and even more delighted to say that he's Bob Tomlinson, whose work I'm sure you know from such hit series as *No Kidding, O'Reilly and Truly, Last, But Not Least* and, last but not least, that smashing show set in a municipal rubbish dump, *Hold Your Nose and Think of England!* From that list of credits, I don't need to tell you that Bob certainly knows his stuff when it comes to sit com!

I can't think that Bob's going to want to make major changes to the schedule, but I'm sure you'll hear in plenty of time if any of your calls are different. I look forward to seeing you at the readthrough next Monday, 4th June, and am confident that, after this rather unfortunate start, we are going to have a really exciting and successful series.

With the warmest good wishes,

Yours sincerely,

Peter

PETER LIPSCOMBE

Producer *The Strutters*

The payphone on the landing at Hereford Road rang the morning Charles received the letter. The various Swedes were out at their various Swedish occupations, so he answered it.

'Hello, Charles, it's Walter.'

'Oh, hello. How are things?'

'So-so. Look, I hope you don't mind my ringing, but I wanted to pick your brains . . .'

'You're welcome to anything you can find there.'

'It's a slightly ticklish thing, actually. I read in the paper about that poor boy's terrible accident . . . you know, your director. Obviously I was terribly shocked, but I couldn't help thinking, you know, the way one does, that that must leave your series without a director. So I thought I might give Peter Lipscombe a buzz and see what gives, but I thought I'd check with you first, just to make sure nothing's been sorted out yet.'

Charles didn't like the drift of the conversation, and said rather shortly, 'I've just heard. We've got a new director.'

'Oh. Who?'

'Bob . . . Tomlinson I think it was.'

'Ah, yes. He's never out of work. Yes, of course. He would be free. He was going to do that series about the dance band called *Hands Off My Maracas,* but it's been cancelled because of problems with the Musicians' Union. Oh well, never mind . . . We must meet up for a drink again sometime, maybe.'

'Sure.'

'And you will let me know if you hear anything coming up, won't you?'

'Yes. Of course.'

Charles went back into his room feeling depressed. Of course Walter had to follow up any job possibility that might emerge, but it was unpleasant to hear him reduced to the role of professional vulture. For a moment suspicion of Walter returned. Certainly he was someone who might hope to gain from Scott Newton's death, and he'd made no secret of his resentment of the young man's success.

But there were many arguments against casting Walter in the role of the director's murderer. The first, and most potent, was that he hadn't been at the scene of the crime.

Short of introducing a conspiracy theory or the use of a hired killer, there was no way he could have toppled the flower urn which had caused Scott's death.

And why should anyone want Scott dead? He had seemed pleasant enough, not the sort to raise instant antipathy like Sadie. Just an ambitious young television director with money problems.

Mind you, the money problems seemed to have resolved themselves. The new clothes, the new car ... Charles's mind did a little spurt. Suppose Scott had witnessed the first murder and blackmailed the killer, thus providing a motive for his own death ... ? Hmm, there might be something there, but there was a distinct lack of hard evidence.

And, anyway, was there even a murder to investigate? There seemed no real reason to think that the young man was the victim of anything more sinister than an accident. The police, who had made extensive investigations at the scene of his death, seemed satisfied with this solution. And, after all, a young man, flushed with success after a good day's filming, showing off a powerful and unfamiliar car, was unlikely to be concentrating much on his driving. And the urn of flowers could have fallen of its own accord. Charles knew from having leant against one that they weren't fixed, just balanced on the wall.

Yes, it *could* have fallen of its own accord. But it was a substantial piece of terracotta and there had been no wind. Perhaps a bird could have flown into it or a rabbit or something brushed against it ... or maybe the vibrations of one of the passing cars had dislodged it, but it all seemed pretty unlikely.

Maybe one of the cars had scraped against the wall and bumped the urn off ... But logic was against that too. Whereas one could imagine that the ancient Barton Rivers, at the wheel of his huge Bentley, might be less than secure on the tight turns of the drive, he and Aurelia had not been the last people to go down it. Bernard Walton had followed them and, apart from the fact that he must have known every curve of the approach to his house perfectly, he was unlikely to scrape the gleaming surface of his precious Rolls. And he wouldn't have been able to drive over the urn if Barton's Bentley had dislodged it before him.

So either it just fell, or someone deliberately moved it. And if it had been deliberately moved, it must have happened just after Bernard's Rolls had driven past.

If it was murder, and if it had been planned, then the perpetrator was likely to be someone who knew the layout of Bernard's grounds, someone who had been there before. The list included Bernard himself, obviously, and, from what they had said during the day, Aurelia and Barton and Peter Lipscombe. Presumably the unfortunate Scott had also been down on a recce to check the location, and who knew how many people would have accompanied him? Certainly the designer, certainly the Location Manager, possibly Janie Lewis, the PA, possibly dozens of other people. That was the trouble with a crime committed in television — there were always so many people about, it was difficult to reduce lists of suspects.

Charles concentrated, and tried to remember where everyone had been at the moment of Bernard Walton's departure in the Rolls. The conjectural saboteur of the urn need not have been in a car; he, or she, could have walked down the hill and moved it. But the picture didn't come back to him with any clarity. He just remembered a lot of people milling about, clearing up; he couldn't place individuals.

No, he came back to one fact: if the urn was moved in order to cause an accident, then the person with the best background knowledge and the best opportunity to do it was Bernard Walton.

And it was also Bernard Walton with whom Sadie Wainwright had had a blazing row just before her death.

But why? Why should a highly successful television and theatre star hazard everything by committing murder? Charles supposed that if *The Strutters* had been being made at the expense of *What'll the Neighbours Say?*, then Bernard might be seen to have a motive for sabotaging production of the new series, so that it would have to be cancelled and replaced with the older one. But that motivation didn't work, because the options on the next series of *What'll the Neighbours Say?* had been taken up and, though Bernard didn't know that at the time of Sadie's death, he certainly did when Scott died. Nope, it didn't work.

But, as a theory, it did contain one attractive element, and that was the idea of sabotage to the production. If the violence was directed against the whole series rather than individuals, then the random nature of the murder schemes made more sense. Maybe the saboteur had fixed the railing on the fire escape to injure Sadie Wainwright *or anyone else* connected with *The Strutters* pilot. The dislodged urn, too, might have been a random act of violence.

This idea answered a doubt that had been nagging at Charles ever since Scott's death. Any theory that assumed murder directed specifically at the young director also assumed an enormous amount of luck. There was no guarantee that Scott was going to be the next person down the hill after Bernard. He might well have chosen to leave last of all and demonstrate the powers of his Porsche by overtaking everyone else on the motorway back to London. Even if the murderer could have predicted the bet with Peter Lipscombe, he couldn't have known that the producer would offer the opportunity for the director to go first. (Unless of course the producer *were* the murderer . . . But no, that was a blind alley; it was Scott who had suggested the race.)

And, as well as having no guarantee who his victim would be, the conjectural murderer had no guarantee that he would murder anyone. A more prudent driver than Scott Newton might have been going slowly enough to stop safely when he saw his path obstructed. And, even given Scott's precipitous speed, he might well have survived his descent on to the main road. No murderer, however much of a criminal mastermind, could have arranged the simultaneous arrival of a Spanish juggernaut to finish off his victim.

So, if any crimes had been committed, it looked as if they were just random sabotage. And the only person who had ever had a motive for such actions, Bernard Walton, had had his motive removed by the guarantee of a new series of *What'll the Neighbours Say?*

Unless, of course, the acts of sabotage were the work of a psychopath. Oh dear, Charles did hope not. Psychopathic crimes offered no prospect of satisfaction; if their motivation was without reason, then no amount of reasoning was going to provide a solution to them.

So what was he left with? Two deaths. Both, according to police findings, accidental. And nothing to make him disagree with those findings except for a few ambiguous overheard words relating to the first one.

All he could do was watch and listen, and wait to see if anything else happened.

On Monday, June 4th, Charles arrived at the Paddington Jewish Boys' Club for the first *Strutters* readthrough, and found Peter Lipscombe predictably cooing over Aurelia Howarth. She appeared just to have given him a brown paper parcel.

'Of course I'll read them, Dob love, of course I will.'

'I don't know, I just think there might be something there, darling. They're old-fashioned, but might adapt into a rather jolly series. Just an instinct I have about them.'

'And when have your dramatic instincts ever been wrong?' asked the producer with a sycophantic laugh.

Charles moved over to sit beside George Birkitt, who was reading the *Sun*. 'How's tricks, as the white rabbit said to the conjuror?'

George brandished the newspaper. 'Look at this — bloody Bernard Walton all over it.'

Charles glanced at the page. 'MY FIRST DATE — In our series of the Famous with Two Left Feet, BERNARD WALTON, hilarious star of TV's *What'll the Neighbours Say?* describes the visit to the pictures that went riotously wrong . . .' He didn't read any further. There was a half-page picture of Bernard, pulling one of the gauche expressions that was a feature of the character he played in the sit com (and indeed of every other character he played; whatever the part, he always gave the same performance).

Charles shrugged. 'So what?'

'I don't know. I just get a bit sick of it,' George Birkitt complained. 'I mean, you just can't get away from him. He's always doing all these bloody interviews, and popping up on quiz shows and all that rubbish. All the *Blankety-Blanks* and *Star Games* and *Celebrity Squares* when that was around. Or he's opening supermarkets or being photographed at premieres . . .'

'I agree, it must be hell. But that's the life he's chosen.

One of the penalties of being a star, you have to be on show all of the time.'

'Yes,' said George, with a tinge of wistfulness.

'Surely you don't want to get involved in all that, do you?'

'Good Lord, no,' he protested. 'No, no, I value my privacy. I'm the last person to want to become a public property. No, no, I was just thinking from the financial point of view. I mean, there is quite a bit of money in all those spin-off things. And I think, you know, if you get the chance to do them, well, you shouldn't turn them down from high-minded principles about the sanctity of your art. You should take advantage of whatever's going.'

'Oh, I agree.'

'And, if there's money going for all that sort of rubbish, I don't see why it should always go to the same circle of boring professional personalities with heads too big for their bodies. Because, to be quite frank, Charles ...' George Birkitt lowered his voice, 'I wouldn't mind a little more money. They're getting me damned cheap for this series. Okay, I know it's the first time I've had my name above the title — as if I cared about things like that, for God's sake — but they are still getting me damned cheap. No, if they want to do another series after this lot, I'm afraid they'll find my agent in more of a negotiating mood. It's not that one wants a huge amount of money, it's just that one doesn't want to be undervalued.'

Further demonstration of George Birkitt's unwillingness to fall into a star stereotype was prevented by the arrival of *The Strutters'* new director. Bob Tomlinson, the man who certainly knew his stuff when it came to sit com, proved to be a thickset individual in his fifties whose appearance behind a market barrow would have been less remarkable than behind a television control desk. He was dressed in a shiny blue suit and wore an expression of belligerent boredom.

'Okay,' he said. 'Let's sit down and read this rubbish.'

'Bob!' cried Peter Lipscombe heartily. 'Sure you'd like to be introduced to everyone, wouldn't you?'

'I'll get to know them soon enough in rehearsal,' said Bob Tomlinson, and sat down.

'But you haven't worked with Dob Howarth, have you?' Peter Lipscombe persisted.

'No.'

'Well, do allow me to introduce you to our lovely leading lady.'

Bob Tomlinson looked up briefly. 'Hello. Right, PA got the watch ready? Let's start reading.'

Peter Lipscombe intervened again. 'Er, yes. Just a moment, Bob. If I could say a few words . . .'

'Why?'

'Well, er, as producer, I would like to —'

'Oh yeah, I forgot you were producer. All right, be quick. I'll get myself a coffee.' And Bob Tomlinson got up and walked across to the coffee machine, while Peter Lipscombe started his pep-talk.

'Right, first let me say now nice it is to see you all looking so well. Now we've all had a horrible shock and there's no use pretending what happened didn't happen, but what we've all got to do is to put it behind us and look ahead, just remember what a jolly exciting series this is going to be. Now, because of circumstances, we've lost a couple of days filming, but we'll be able to pick them up in the course of our schedule. And, incidentally, I'd like to warn you now that I've just received Script Number Six from Rod and that's going to involve some of you in a night's filming. We'll let you know the date as soon as it's been sorted out, but I thought you'd like to know.

'So . . . here we all are and by this time next week we'll have recorded the first episode — second, if we include the pilot — of this really exciting new series — *The Strutters!* Let me tell you, ladies and gentlemen —'

'Have you finished?' asked Bob Tomlinson, returning with his cup of coffee.

'Well, er, yes, I, er, um . . .'

'Okay, read from the top. Start the watch, girl.'

Maybe it was the inhibiting expression of boredom on the director's face, or perhaps it was just that the script was inferior to the pilot episode, but the readthrough didn't seem very funny. Peter Lipscombe and Tilly Lake provided their usual sycophantic laughter for the first few pages, but soon faded to silence.

As the pay-off to the episode was spoken, Bob Tomlinson turned to Janie. 'How long?'

'Part One: 10-17, Part Two: 9-41,' she supplied

efficiently. 'Making a total of 19-58.'

'That's near enough.' Bob rose with the enthusiasm of a man about to put three coats of paint on a forty-foot wall. 'Let's block it.'

Peter Lipscombe raised a hand to intervene. 'Um, just a few points before you do that. Debbi, that line you have on 1-7, where you say, "No, I'm not that sort of girl" . . . could you —'

''Ere, what is this?' asked Bob Tomlinson, with all the anger of a barrow-boy who's arrived at market to find someone else on his pitch. 'I'm the director of this show. I give the bleeding artists notes.'

Peter Lipscombe didn't want a scene. His voice took on a mollifying tone. 'Yes, of course, Bob, of course. I wonder if you'd mention to Debbi that I think one way — not by any means the only way, but *one* way of delivering that line would be to emphasise the "that". "I'm not *that* sort of girl." I think it points up the joke.'

'All right,' Bob Tomlinson conceded. 'Which one of you's Debbi? Right, on that line, could you hit the "that"? Okay, let's get this bloody show blocked.'

'I've got a point, Bob,' said the colourless voice of Rod Tisdale.

'And who the hell are you? Another bloody producer?'

'No, Bob, this is our writer, Rod Tisdale.'

Bob Tomlinson glowered. 'I don't like writers round my rehearsal rooms.'

Rod Tisdale showed no signes of having heard this. 'It's Page 3 of Part Two.'

'Oh, don't bother me with bloody details on the script. Tell the producer.'

'Peter,' said Rod Tisdale obediently, 'on that page, I think the line, "I can't stand it any longer" would probably be better as "I can't stick it out any longer." You know, probably pick up the laugh on the double meaning."

'Yes, nice thinking, Rod. Um, Bob, Rod's had rather a good idea, I think. On Page 3 of Part Two, wondering if we could change "I can't stand it any longer" to "I can't stick it out any longer" . . .'

'Change it. See if I care.'

'No, but I don't want us to force it on you. We all want to be in agreement on things. So do say what you'd like.'

'I'd like you and the bloody writer to clear out and let me get on with this rubbish.'

As rehearsals progressed, Charles found his respect for Bob Tomlinson increasing. He realised that the director's manner was not just rudeness for its own sake, but a way of getting on with the job quickly. And his contempt for the material he was directing (a feeling for which Charles found in himself considerable sympathy) did not seem to make the performances any worse. Nor did it lower the morale of the production; after the agonising of Scott Newton over every comma, the more practical approach was quite a relief. The atmosphere in the rehearsal room was rather jolly.

Bob Tomlinson just got on with the job and didn't waste time with socialising or toadying to his stars. He was an efficient organiser and ensured that every part of the production came together at the right time. He was a good example of the huge value of competence in television. Flair may have its place, but flair is not always coupled with efficiency and, given the choice between a director with flair and one with competence, many actors would opt for the security of the latter.

Certainly the cast of *The Strutters* didn't seem put out by the offhand manner of their new director. They seemed to respect his lack of obsequiousness. It made them more equal, a group of people who had come together to get on with a job of work. Aurelia Howarth, used to cosseting and cotton-woolling from generations of producers, seemed totally unworried by Bob Tomlinson's directness and his undisguised lack of interest in the welfare of Cocky.

The atmosphere between director and producer remained. The fact was that Bob Tomlinson was not used to working to a producer. For many years he had combined the roles, and his agent had ensured that the final credit read: 'Produced and Directed by Bob Tomlinson'. It was only because of the last-minute nature of his booking on *The Strutters* when his other series was cancelled that he found himself in this unusual position.

But he didn't let it worry him. He didn't let anything worry him. *The Strutters* was just another three months of well-paid work, and soon he'd be on to something else.

The secret of Bob Tomlinson's success and his formidable track record in sit com was his ability not to let anything get to him. He was the first person Charles had met in that world who seemed to have an accurate estimate of the value and importance of the product.

He continued to be cheerfully rude to Peter Lipscombe and continued to allow no notes to be given directly from the producer to the artists. So there were more conversations in which people with a common language talked through an interpreter. But Peter Lipscombe's role, which under Scott Newton's inexperienced regime had increased, dwindled back to grinning a lot, asking everyone if everything was okay and buying drinks. Which was, after all, what he did best.

The actual recording of Episode One (or Episode Two, if you counted the pilot) of *The Strutters* did not go particularly well. This was in no way due to Bob Tomlinson's direction. There was, after all, only one way to shoot a Rod Tisdale script, and that was the way he did it. All that was wrong with the evening was that the script was slightly inferior, and after all the euphoric generalisations about new eras in comedy which had followed the pilot, anti-climax was inevitable.

After the recording, Charles overheard a conversation between the writer and director. Rod Tisdale, in a voice that almost betrayed some emotion, asked, 'How d'you think it went?'

Bob Tomlinson shrugged. 'All right. How does any sit com go?'

Rod Tisdale shook his head. 'I don't know. I reckoned there were sixty-eight jokes in that script. We only got fifty-three laughs.'

'It'll look fine after the sound-dub.'

'You mean you'll add the laughs?'

'You bet I will. By the time I've finished, you won't be able to tell the difference between this and a really funny show.'

'I've always resisted having laughs dubbed on to my shows.'

'Sod what you've always resisted, son. I'm directing this show and I'll do it my way.'

Which was of course the way it would be done.

Charles decided to go up to the bar in the lift. (Though no one actually mentioned it, the fire escape had been used much less since Sadie's death.) He had changed with his customary rapidity out of his top half (Reg the golf club barman's legs, after their brief airing on film, had once again retreated to proper obscurity), and reckoned only Peter Lipscombe would have beaten him to the bar. Where he could once again demonstrate his skill in buying drinks.

There was an argument going on outside the lift. A small balding man with glasses, who carried a duffle bag and wore a thin checked sports jacket and a yellow nylon shirt, was being moved on by a uniformed commissionaire.

'No, I'm sorry, sir, show's over. I have to clear all the audience out of the building. Now come along, please.'

'But she will see me, she will. She always does.'

'No, I'm sorry, sir, I've got to clear the building. So, if you don't mind . . . If it's an autograph you want, you're welcome to wait outside the main door until the artists come out.'

'I don't want her autograph. I've got her autograph a thousand times over. I've got authographed programmes of every show she's ever been in. I've collected them all.'

'Sorry, sir, I must —'

'No, listen, my name's Romney Kirkstall. She knows me. Really. You just tell her I'm here and —'

'She know you were coming tonight?'

'No, she didn't actually, but she's always glad to see me. I come to all the *What'll the Neighbours* . . . recordings and —'

'If the lady's not expecting you, sir, I'm afraid I must ask you to —'

'No, really, she will want to see me!

Before the commissionaire could produce further verbal or physical arguments, the truth of Romney Kirkstall's assertion was proved by the zephyrous arrival of Aurelia Howarth, saying, 'Romney, darling, how good of you to come!'

'You're lucky I'm still here, Dob,' said the little man. 'This . . . gentleman was doing his best to throw me out.'

'I'm sorry, Miss Howarth,' the commissionaire apologised

74

sheepishly. 'I didn't know who he was. We get a lot of types wanting to worry the stars and that. I thought he might be some kind of freak.'

The wildness of Kirkstall's appearance justified that supposition, but Aurelia cooed lightly, 'No, no, Romney's my most loyal fan.'

The lift arrived at that moment, so she continued. 'Come on, darling, let's go up and have a drink. Sorry about the mix-up.'

Charles went into the lift with them and they all arrived together in the bar. Where, predictably enough, Peter Lipscombe bought them all drinks. And he did do it very well.

Gerlad Venables had once again come to the recording and Charles met him in the bar. The actor was becoming suspicious of the solicitor's constant appearances at West End Television. Though he always claimed disingenuously he had just come to see the show, Gerald was notorious for investing in the lucrative areas of show business, and Charles wouldn't have been at all surprised to discover he had a stake in the company. He seemed to know everyone altogether too well to be a mere casual visitor. And his constant discussions with W.E.T.'s Head of Contracts suggested more than idle conversation.

But Charles never expected to have his suspicions confirmed. Gerlad was masonically secretive about his investments.

'Still think we're on to a winner?' he asked ironically, after Peter Lipscombe had bought Gerald a drink too.

'Oh yes,' asserted the solicitor confidently. 'Minor hiccup tonight, but it'll be fine. Yes, this series is going to make the autumn schedules look very healthy. What with this and Wragg and Bowen, the BBC'll be knocked for six.'

Gerald was talking so exactly like Peter Lipscombe that Charles once again suspected him of complicity with the company's management. He seemed to know altogether too much.

But Gerald's interest in television was subsidiary to his interest in criminal investigation. He had helped Charles on one or two cases in the past and was evidently avid for more.

'Well? Two suspicious deaths now. What do you make of it, bud?'

'A coincidence of two accidents, I think.'

'Oh, come on, you can do better than that.'

'I don't know. I've thought it through a lot, but I can't seem to get any line on it at all. Either there are two totally unrelated crimes, or only one crime and one accident, or no crimes. I can't get any consistent motivation for anyone.'

And he gave Gerald a summary of his thinking to date. 'The only person for whom I've got even a wisp of motivation,' he concluded, 'is dear old Bernard Walton. If he thought the future of his own series was threatened by *The Strutters*, then he would in theory have a motive to sabotage the show. And, if you think on those lines, it becomes significant that the two people who have died have nothing to do with *What'll the Neighbours Say?* I mean, say Aurelia or George had gone, then that might jeopardise the future of the series, but as it is, there's nothing to stop it going ahead. As indeed — and here's the one fact that makes the whole theory crumble in ruins about my ears — it *is* going ahead. I'll have to think of something else.'

'I've got news for you, Charles,' Gerald announced portentously.

'What?'

'I was just talking to the Head of Contracts. The proposed series of *What'll the Neighbours Say?* has been cancelled.'

'It can't have been. The artists' options have been taken up.'

'Oh, sure. But they're all going to be paid off. Head of Contracts has been ringing round the agents today. Were you optioned for the series, by the way?'

'No. They just did an availability check. Said it wasn't definite that Reg the golf club barman would be a regular character.'

Gerald grimaced. 'If your agent was worth his commission, he'd have got some sort of contract out of them. Who is your agent, by the way?'

'Maurice Skellern.'

'Oh. Say no more.'

'But just a minute, Gerald, they wouldn't pay everyone'

'Why not? Happens all the time.'

'But it's a huge amount of money.'

'A huge amount of money for the actors involved, maybe. A very nice little pay-off for doing nothing. But, as a percentage of the budget of a major television production, it's peanuts, really. So long as you actually keep a show out of the studio, you're still saving money. In fact, there are producers who have built up considerable reputations by keeping shows out of studios.'

Once again Gerald was showing more than a layman's knowledge of the workings of television, but Charles didn't comment. Instead, he said, 'Anyway, even if that has happened, and I still don't quite see why it has . . .'

'Nigel Frisch has lost confidence in the series. And they need the studio dates for Wragg and Bowen.'

'Okay, but coming back to our little problem of a murder motivation, we're no further advanced. If the artists' agents were only told about the cancellation today —'

'Yes, most of them were. But Bernard Walton, because he was the star, was given the honour of knowing the bad news before anyone else. Nigel Frisch, who, whatever else one may say about him, is never one to shirk responsibility, rang Bernard personally.'

'When?'

'Last Tuesday.'

The day before Scott Newton's death.

CHAPTER SEVEN

The atmosphere at the Paddington Jewish Boys' Club Hall for the readthrough the following morning was distinctly subdued. Partly, this was because the previous night's recording had been less than successful, but there was also a communal consciousness that they were now all into a weekly turnaround of shows; they would have to work harder and there would be less time for anything else. And there were some sore heads. The very human tendency to have a few drinks and go out for a meal after a recording that finishes at ten rarely takes account of a ten-thirty call the next morning.

George Birkitt was the only one who seemed cheerful. His agent had come to the recording and told him about the *What'll the Neighbours Say?* pay-off. Not only did this give him financial encouragement, because the contracted fees for thirteen programmes came to a very considerable amount, it also seemed a promising augury for *The Strutters* series. The company was clearly backing the new show at the expense of the old one. And, though he didn't quite say it, he reckoned that meant they thought George Birkitt was now a more bankable star than Bernard Walton. 'The other thing is,' he confided to Charles, 'it means I'll be able to take some other work. My agent keeps having calls from casting directors offering quite nice stuff, but always has to turn it down, saying, no, sorry, love, he's under contract to W.E.T. Exclusive contracts have their advantages, but they do restrict your movement.'

Charles Paris, whose experience of exclusive contracts was small nodded wisely.

But George was the only one in a sunny mood. Even Aurelia, whose diaphanous charm rarely varied, seemed distracted. Apparently it was something to do with Cocky, who had been sick during the night and had to have the vet summoned. The lack of sleep this disturbance had caused made the actress look slightly less ageless than usual. Charles was more aware of the strains a television series must impose on a woman in her seventies.

And she was obviously worried about the dog. Throughout the read-through, she kept going across to his little basket to check on his welfare. 'If anything happened to Cocky,' she said, 'I don't know what I'd do.'

Janie Lewis was also less than her beaming efficient self. Dark circles under her eyes suggested she hadn't had any sleep the night before and a strained atmosphere between her and one of the regular cast, Nick Coxhill, suggested why. Charles once again thought he might continue his desultory pursuit of her, but his first overture was met with the sharp retort that she was henceforth to be known as Jay, and that she was busy.

Tilly Lake emoted round the rehearsal room, implying

enough sighing heartaches to keep a romantic novelist in business for a decade. Charles, rather cheekily, asked her whether she'd heard from Trevor Howard or Laurence Olivier about playing the part of Colonel Strutter's friend in Episode Five.

'Both got other commitments,' she said elegiacally. 'Otherwise, of course ... Still, I'm not downhearted. Going to continue to aim high. Such a smashing script, after all, lovely part. I've been reading it and I think the character might be rather younger than I first thought. So I think I might try for an Alan Bates, or a Michael York maybe ... or a Derek Jacobi. Keep away from the obvious, anyway, the Toby Roots of this life. Nothing against him, but you know what I mean.'

Charles mumbled some ambivalent response.

'Casting so easily becomes predictable, so one always admires the people in television who don't do the obvious. I mean, have you heard, on this programme for the elderly, they haven't gone for the boring competent sort of presenter like Robert Carton. They've chosen Ian Reynolds, who's nearly eighty.'

'Yes, I heard that.'

'Well, isn't that inventive?' And people sometimes say casting isn't a creative business.' She laughed tragically, setting up a ripply through the feathers of her hat.

'What does Bob Tomlinson think about your ideas of casting?'

'Oh, he doesn't care. He just told me to get on with it.'

That was Bob Tomlinson's great quality, the ability to get on with it and to delegate. But he wasn't slapdash. He had his own standards, as was apparent when he clapped his hands for attention.

'Before we start this readthrough, got another filming date for your diaries. This Friday, the 15th. We're meant to be rehearsing here, but if we get our skates on, we can miss a day.'

'Where's the location?' asked Debbi Hartley.

'Back at Bernard Walton's place.'

'But I thought we'd done all that.'

'Got to do it again.'

'Why?' Peter Lipscombe's producer's instinct picked up the implication of extra expense.

'Because I saw the rushes this morning of what was done last week, and it's all bloody terrible. I wouldn't have film of that quality in one of my shows.'

'What's wrong with it?'

'It's all bloody arty-farty. All shot over people's shoulders or up their trouser-leg. Every new director's first day with a film camera. Just bloody wanking. I don't know what that little tit thought he was up to.'

Peter Lipscombe still seemed more worried about the prospect of spending money than any disrespect to the dead. 'Are you sure there isn't any of it you can use?'

'Bloody certain.'

'Well, look, I'll have to talk to the Cost Planners about this. And then to Film Department to see if they can find us a day to —'

'I've done all that. Don't you bloody listen? It's all set up for this Friday.'

'Oh.' Peter Lipscombe had one more try. 'I'm sure the film can't be that bad . . .'

'It's self-indulgent crap. Totally wrong for this show. Don't ever forget, what we're making here is just a second-rate sit com, not bloody Ingmar Bergman.'

And so — not that there had ever been any doubt that he would — Bob Tomlinson won the day. All of the people who had been present at Scott Newton's death were to be reassembled at the scene of the crime.

Charles wondered if Bernard Walton would also be there.

In the Birthday Honours, announced the next day, Aurelia Howarth was made a Dame of the British Empire. This caused considerable excitement at the Paddington Jewish Boys' Club, which was invaded by newspaper reporters, and even had a sycophantic royal visit from Nigel Frisch.

His legs once again encased in Reg the golf club barman's alien trousers, Charles Paris went through his second day's filming at Bernard Walton's house. If doing it once had been boring, doing it twice was excruciating. The only improvement on the previoous occasion was that Bob Tomlinson moved a lot faster than Scott Newton. While the younger man had spent hours composing every shot, the older one just got the camera lined up and went ahead. He had a cameraman with a comparably prosaic approach to the job. The inestimable Midge Trumper had shared Scott Newton's concern to make every frame a Rembrandt; the new man's only worry seemed to be making sure that there was film in the camera.

The result was that the men in lumberjack shirts' prospects of going into overtime faded fast. By the time they broke for lunch (pâté de foie gras, steak au poivre and raspberries with — thanks to the intervention of the Union representative — a rather good 1973 Mouton Cadet), only four set-ups and a couple of establishing shots remained to be done. All Dame Aurelia Howarth's scenes had been completed, and she and Barton Rivers had already set off in the Bentley back to London. She still looked very tired and would no doubt benefit from a half-day's rest. The excitements of all the congratulations on her award must have added to her exhautsion.

But, though the progress of the filming was rapid and efficient, Charles made little or no progress in the business of criminal investigation. He did wander down the drive to the point where Scott's Porsche had skidded off, but the scene of the accident told him nothing new.

Bernard Walton must have had efficient staff, because most traces of the car's descent had been erased. Walls had been repaired, broken shrubs replaced, and scarred lawn returfed. Only the difference in colour between the old grass and the new bore witness to the spectacle of the previous week.

Charles once again weighed one of the urns in his hands. Their centre of gravity was high, so it wouldn't take much of a nudge to shift them, but, even so, they were heavy and it would require more than a gust of wind to do the job.

He looked around the area. Maybe some vital clue remained, maybe the vital stub of a cigarette only available from a small shop in Burlington Arcade, maybe the unmistakable outline of a shoe with callipers, maybe the return half of a railway ticket to Auchtermuchty ... But he was not optimistic of finding anything. People on the whole rarely leave clues to where they have been. And, if there had been any, he felt sure the police's more professional searches would have revealed them.

No, there was only one line of investigation open to him. And he was prevented from pursuing that by the absence of his chief suspect. Bernard Walton wasn't there.

He arrived just as the day's filming was finished, at about three o'clock. The Rolls scrunched to a halt on the gravel. Bernard's powder-blue leisure-wear and the gleaming leather bag of clubs he removed from the back of the car revealed that he had been on the golf course. His breath revealed that he had also been in the bar.

He greeted Charles warmly. 'Is Dame Dob around?' he asked.

'No. Her bits were finished early. She went off about lunchtime.'

'Ah.' Bernard Walton hesitated. He had had a hospitable urge, but now he knew Aurelia and Barton weren't there, didn't know what to do with it. 'Are you through, too?'

'Yes. It's all done. The magic words, "It's a wrap," have been spoken.'

'Uh-huh.' Bernard was still undecided. But only for a moment. 'Look, would you like to come in and have a drink?'

'That's very kind, but I think the coach'll be going back shortly and . . .'

'Don't worry about that. I've got to drive up to Town later. Got to go on some radio chat show. Live at ten o'clock — ugh. Bloody inconvenient, but I'd better do it.'

'Well, in that case . . .' A snag. 'But I'm in costume.'

'Oh tell them you'll take it in tomorrow.'

'They won't like it.'

They didn't, but Charles was too determined to grab his chance of talking to Bernard to worry about the affronted flouncing of a dresser.

They sat by the window of Bernard's sitting room with glasses of brandy and watched the cavalcade of buses and cars depart.

'How's it going?' asked the star of *What'll the Neighbours Say?*

'Hard to judge, really. I'm not very good at assessing comedy, least of all this sort of stuff.'

'I think it'll probably be very successful,' Bernard condescended.

'Hmm. Of course, it's got off to rather a disturbed start . . .'

But the opportunity to talk about Scott's death was ignored. 'You've heard they're not going to proceed with *What'll the Neighbours . . .*?'

Charles nodded. 'Still, nice big pay-off, I gather.'

'Yes.' Bernard's tone did not suggest that the money was a great comfort. 'Oh well, maybe I should go back to the theatre. Might get a job in rep. at Cardiff,' he suggested ruefully.

This reference to their first meeting released a variety of reminiscences. Charles played along. He wanted to bring the conversation round to the deaths of Sadie and Scott, but he had to do it gently. Also, there was something about Bernard's manner, the way he had buttonholed Charles and insisted on his staying, that suggested he might want to unburden himself of some confidence. But it mustn't be hurried.

It was about half-past five when Bernard suggested they should leave for Town. 'I have a call to make on the way. It won't take long. I hope you don't mind.'

Charles didn't. His social claendar was as empty as ever. Whether he arrived back at Hereford Road at seven or midnight or indeed three a.m. made little difference. He had had a vague intention to ring Frances that evening, but it'd keep.

The call Bernard had to make proved to be at a home for spastics. Charles said, no, he didn't mind coming in with him.

It was a strange experience, prompting mixed reactions. On one level, Charles knew that it was a carefully-engineered public relations exercise. He felt sure that Bernard had made his call before in other more eminent company. After all, there was little point in impressing Charles Paris with the great star's big-heartedness. They had known each other too long. Charles knew the kind of calculation that went into everything Bernard did, and had a shrewd suspicion Bernard knew he knew.

On the other hand, it was undeniable that, whatever his motive, the star was doing good. The expressions on the distorted faces of the children he addressed spoke their welcome. And his familiarity with names and interests vouched for the regularity of such visits. As did the gratitude of the nursing staff.

Charles was brought back to a conclusion that he had often reached before: that a good action remains a good action, whatever its motivation. The fact that Bernard was making capital out of his work with the handicapped, the fact that he was very deliberately supplying a lack of natural humanity, that he was consciously building up an image of caring, and quite possibly scoring points to be recognised in some future Honours List, did not detract from the pleasure that he brought to the objects of his manufactured concern.

Charles found himslelf disarmed by this discovery. Having seen Bernard in action on the hospital visit was not going to make it any easier to challenge him over the deaths of Sadie Wainwright and Scott Newton (though he knew that, if Bernard had an inkling of his suspicions, the star was quite capable of deliberately fostering such a mood of doubt).

The visit only took half an hour. The matron and a few giggling nurses saw them to the main door. 'Haven't seen you on the television so much recently, Mr. Walton,' commented the matron.

He grinned. 'Ah no. Have to ration myself. Don't want the public to get bored with me.'

'Oh, I'm sure that wouldn't happen.'

'All too easily, matron, all too easily.'

'I bet you've got another big series coming up soon, haven't you?'

Bernard Walton laid his finger slyly along the side of his nose. 'Big secret, matron, big secret.'

'Ooh, I bet you have something coming up.'

'All,' he announced mysteriously, 'will become clear at the proper time.'

Back in the car, Charles asked the blunt question, 'Have you really got a new series coming up?'

'No,' replied Bernard gloomily, 'but I can't tell them that, can I?'

As they approached London, Bernard asked if he had any plans for the evening. Charles, whose plans rarely aspired beyond a visit to the Montrose, said he hadn't.

'I'd thought of dining at my club, the Greville. Be delighted if you'd join me.'

'Oh, but I . . .' Charles instinctively thought of his usual dress (once dignified by Gerald Venables with the description 'neo-woodcutter'). But no, of course, Reg the barman's blazer and ungiving trousers were quite suitable for dining in a gentleman's club.

So it proved. As they entered the splendid hallway of the Greville, an elderly member, mellowed by alcohol, seized Charles by the hand and confided that he'd always recognise an Old Millingtonian tie and had he heard anything from Stubby Harbottle.

They dined well in a small, darkly panelled room. It was still early and they were alone. As Charles had suspected, Bernard was now in confiding mood. Not only confiding, but morbidly realistic.

'I don't need to tell you, Charles, the news about *'What'll the Neighbours* . . . was pretty serious for me.'

'Oh, something else'll come up,' Charles assured him easily.

Bernard Walton shook his head. 'No sign of it. I need a starring vehicle and there just ain't another one around.'

'Oh, come on. You're not going to be out of work.'

'No, not out of work, but out of the right sort of work. Okay, I can do a few guest appearances on other people's shows, I can do panel games, that sort of stuff, but I need the continuity of my own show. Everything else springs from that. You heard that Matron — 'Haven't seen you on the television so much recently, Mr. Walton.' It doesn't take long for the public to forget a face, you know.

'And, apart from that, there's the money. It takes a few bob to maintain the sort of establishment I do.' Charles could well believe it. 'It isn't just the money for the television series that counts, it's all the other spin-off stuff. You get booked for cabaret or after-dinner speaking or other shows *because* you're seen regularly on the box. And now, it seems, I'm not going to be seen regularly on the box.'

'I'm sure some other series'll come up for you.'

'I hope so. I've been talking to a few writers to see if they've got ideas. I'm prepared to put up development money. I'm trying to get Rod Tisdale. He's the best for my sort of comedy, but he's always got so much work. Still, there's an idea of his that might work out, but it's early days yet. I need another property.'

It was interesting to hear how Bernard thought in properties. He didn't just want a job, he wanted a personal setting for his own personality. It was an attitude to show business which Charles had never found necessary.

But as Bernard talked the precarious nature of his position became clearer. The top-rating series was essential to his operation. Without it, the celebrity bookings would only continue for a short time and he would degenerate into a professional celebrity, a tree without roots, famous for being famous, without any basis of other work to justify his status. The stakes were high and a character with a star complex like Bernard Walton might go to considerable lengths to maintain his position.

He was surprisingly aware of his limitations. 'What worries me about it most, Charles, is that I think this is a symptom. Nigel Frisch stopped *What'll the Neighbours* . . . , saying that there was nowhere left for the series to go. Rod had worked out every possible permutation of the basic situation. Okay, that's true enough, but it's not a reason for cancelling. Almost every sit com continues long after the basic situation's been exhausted. No, I'm afraid that what Nigel was saying was that he reckoned the public's getting sick of me. After all, I do only do one thing, and they may just have had enough of it. If that is the case, then I really have got problems.'

There was a pause. They both drank from their glasses of wine. What Bernard said next took Charles completely by surprise. 'Which is why,' he pronounced slowly, 'I need your help.'

'I'm sorry?'

'I need your help. I need someone involved in *The Strutters* to keep me informed as to how things are going.'

'What?'

'Listen, that series is thriving at the expense of my series. The company's decided they can't do both. That's been obvious since the spin-off was first mooted. They can't give Dob and George Birkitt star billing in one series and then put them back as supports in *What'll the*

'So you've known from the start that they wouldn't make any more of yours?'

'No, no, I thought they'd make more with new neighbours. Pay off Dob and George and introduce a new couple. I talked to Rod Tisdale about it and we worked out a few story-lines. But now they've cancelled the series flat.'

Bernard looked at the light through his wine glass before continuing. *"What'll the Neighbours Say?* will only come back if *The Strutters* doesn't get made.'

Charles nodded, waiting.

'I keep trying to think what could stop it from getting made. The best thing I can think of is if Dob were to die.'

It was spoken very vasually, but Charles felt a cold chill. It seemed incredible that he was with the same man whose philanthropy with the spastics he had witnessed a couple of hours earlier.

'Unfortunately,' Bernard went on, 'though she's the right sort of age to pop off at any moment, she seems remarkably robust. Have to wish for something else. That's why I'm glad you're there in the cast, Charles.'

'Why?'

'Well, I think you owe me a few favours. I mean, I got you the job, after all.'

'Are you asking me to sabotage the show?'

'No, no, no. Nothing as dramatic as that. I just want you to keep me in touch with the production, how it's going, you know. There may be something I can use. I mean, how did this week's recording go, for instance?'

'Not very well.'

'Good. That's exactly the sort of thing I want to hear.'

Charles tried to recover himself. The new direction of the conversation had come as a shock to him. It had confirmed his conjecture about Bernard's motivation, but he had not expected such a direct statement of the situation. 'I suppose then,' he began slowly, 'you must have been pretty pleased to hear about Sadie's death. And Scott's. Both liable to slow down the advance of the series.'

Bernard nodded. 'Yes. Except that neither of them slowed it down enough. No, I'm delighted so far. The series seems to have got off to a very unpropitious start.

But it's not enough. It's still going ahead. I need something a bit more central than those two deaths. A rather more permanent spanner in the works.'

He stumbled a bit over the last sentence and Charles suddenly realised that the star was very drunk. He must have been at the bottle all day, maybe every day since he had heard of his show's cancellation. That would account for his atypical indiscretion and the strangeness of his approach. But it didn't explain away his desire to destroy *The Strutters*. That was real enough.

Simultaneous with Charles's realisation, the power of the drink seemed to get through to Bernard, who looked blearily about him.

'Sadie,' Charles nudged gently.

'Sadie.' The name was repeated without emphasis.

'She came to your dressing room after the pilot . . .'

'Yes.'

'And she called you a bastard . . .'

'Yes.'

'You had an argument and a little later she fell to her death from the fire escape.'

'Yes.'

'What did you argue about?'

Bernard stopped nodding and a look of cunning came into his face. 'I'd complained to the producer about the allocation of dressing rooms. She regarded this as sneaking behind her back.'

'I see. And Scott?'

'Scott drove too fast.'

That was all he got. In a moment Bernard started drinking black coffee, suddenly aware of the state he was in. He clammed up, realising he had said too much already.

But Charles was pleased with what he had heard. There was now no doubt about the strength of Bernard's motivation and his desire to destroy *The Strutters* at any cost. And, though he hadn't confessed to either of the murders, he had been at least enigmatic about them. And he had effectively asked for Charles's help in his sabotage plan.

All that was needed was evidence to link the two deaths to Bernard. At least now Charles had a clear line of investigation. After rounding off the evening at the

Montrose, he went to bed relatively content.

His content was broken the next day at lunchtime when the radio news announced the death of Rod Tisdale, who had been run over by a vehicle which didn't stop.

Not very funny. Minor accidents are funny, fatal accidents aren't. Basic rule of comedy.

More pertinently, Rod Tisdale had already delivered the six scripts he was writing for the series, so his removal did not impede the progress of *The Strutters* in any way.

What was more, he was a person to whom Bernard Walton looked to provide him with a new star vehicle.

And, most galling of all to any theorist trying to see a pattern of murders committed by the star, Rod Tisdale had been killed at nine o'clock the previous evening. At which time the main suspect was sitting in the Greville Club, dining with Charles Paris.

The case was once again wide open.

CHAPTER EIGHT

West End Television Ltd,
W.E.T. House,
235—9 Lisson Avenue,
London NW1 3PQ.
18th June, 1979.

Dear Charles,

I thought I'd just drop everyone a note after recent events to assure them that, in spite of problems you all know about, everything is okay on *The Strutters* front and all of us here are still confident we've got a very exciting property on our hands.

Until recently we weren't certain whether Rod Tisdale was going to write the remaining scripts in the series or not. He was undecided about it. Obviously now the decision has been made for us, and I am delighted to be able to announce to you that the rest of the series will be written by none other than Willy and Samantha Tennison! I'm sure you're familiar with their work from hosts of successful sit coms, but if your memory needs any nudging, let me just mention such series as *Flat Spin, Daisy and Jonathan, Your Turn, Darling, Oh, What a Pair of Au Pairs!* and that charming show set in a cookery college, *Oh, Crumbs!*

Willy and Sam are delightful people and great chums and I'm sure will be absolutely *right* for *The Strutters.* I've asked them to come along to our next readthrough, so that we can all get a chance to meet up.

Thank you, incidentally, for your continuing hard work on the series. We really have got a smashing cast and I think that's one of the most important ingredients in a really exciting show. Let's put our troubles behind us and look forward to the success *The Strutters* is inevitably going to be!

With the warmest good wishes,

Yours sincerely,

Peter

PETER LIPSCOMBE

Producer *The Strutters*

When Bob Tomlinson arrived at the Paddington Jewish Boys' Club Hall for the next readthrough the following Wednesday and found Willy and Sam Tennison holding court, he said he was going out for a sandwich and would come back in half an hour, by which time everyone had better be ready to start work.

The atmosphere of the second readthrough had cleared, and everyone seemed a lot more cheerful. Rod Tisdale's death, apart from shattering Charles Paris's murder theories, had not had much effect. He had been such an unobtrusive person to have around that his absence was hardly remarked at all.

And any void he might have left was more than filled by Willy and Sam Tennison. They were a roly-poly little pair of writers, a married couple who that day affected patchwork shirts and matching yellow jeans. They were awfully affectionate and flirtatious with each other all the time, and talked in a manner very similar to the scripts of their sit coms. Since most of their success had been based on a series of interchangeable shows which dramatised the small happenings of their own lives, this was hardly surprising.

The viewing public knew everything about them. Their student lives in adjacent flats had hit the screen in the hilarious form of *Flat Spin.* The early days of their marriage had been chronicled in the series *Daisy and Jonathan.* The wacky tribulations of having children took comic form as *Your Turn, Darling* and the increasing affluence these scripts brought them provided the basis for *Oh, What a Pair of Au Pairs!* Their revolutionary attempt to do something different with *Oh, Crumbs!* had been weakened by the fact that the catering college where the series was set was run by a couple called Rob and Mona Partridge, who bore a remarkable similarity to all their other couples.

The Tennisons also had a disconcerting habit of always talking as if they were being interviewed and voluntering information that no one had ever asked for.

Peter Lipscombe thought they were wonderful. He laughed constantly at their shared monologue.

'Well, I don't know, darling,' said Willy Tennison.

'Don't know what, darling?' asked Sam Tennison.

'How we're going to get six scripts together in time, darling.'

'Oh, we'll manage somehow, darling. Lots of midnight oil.'

'But is it going to be worth it with the price oil is these days?'

'Oh, I've got a friend who's a sheik.'

'I thought your friend was the milkman.'

'Well, this guy's a kind of milk sheik.'

'You know, people always ask us how we manage to work together all the time, you know, as man and wife. Don't they, darling?'

'They do, darling.'

'And I always say that there are four of us. There's a husband and a wife and a writer and another writer.'

'And never the twain and the twain shall meet.'

'Yes. Or at least one twain never meets the other twain.'

'Otherwise, darling, there'd be a twain crash.'

'Oh, lovely, darling. I'll write that one down.'

While her husband committed the gem to paper, Sam Tennison continued, 'Willy always uses a blue notebook, while I like pink ones. We never go anywhere without our notebooks, do we, darling?'

'Never, darling. Never know when the Muse will strike.'

'As one pussy cat shop steward said to the other.'

'Oh, darling, that's another one for the book.'

Charles prayed for the return of Bob Tomlinson. He also mentally fabricated a new series which would chronicle the remainder of Willy and Sam Tennison's lives if he had his way. There'd be *Mum's The Word!* for when their tongues were cut out, *There's a Funny Thong!* for when they were garrotted, and, to cover their funerals, *We're Only Here for the Bier!*

Eventually, Bob Tomlinson and belligerent sanity returned.

'Hello, Bob, I'm Sam . . .'

'And I'm Willy . . .'

'Shut up.'

'We're your new writers.'

'Are you? Well, I don't want you round my rehearsal rooms. Send your scripts in by post. You've already wasted enough time this morning. We've got a tight schedule. We're losing two days' rehearsal with the filming we've got to pick up. Incidentally, everyone, the overnight shoot for Ep. Six is fixed for Thursday fortnight. 5th July. Okay, read!'

'But, Sam and I had hoped —'

'But, Willy and I had hoped —'

'Didn't you hear me? Piss off.'

He was a good man, that Bob Tomlinson, thought Charles.

The overnight filming Bob had mentioned was for an insert into the last *Strutters* script Rod Tisdale wrote. In fact, it was the last full script of any sort that he wrote, but anyone who searched through its fabric for some final message from the writer to the world would have been disappointed. All he would have found was a predictable plot, dressed up with sixty-seven familiar jokes, fifty-two of which were destined to receive laughs from the studio audience and the remaining fifteen to have artificial ones imposed in the dubbing suite. Not a great memorial to a human being (which is what Rod Tisdale must have been, though he never gave any sign of it).

Charles had found out as much as he could about the

writer's death, but there was not a lot. His relaxed rehearsal schedule (given a pragmatist like Bob Tomlinson as director, fourteen lines and two moves didn't take long to perfect) allowed him time to go to the inquest, but information seemed to be scarce.

Rod Tisdale had lived in a block of flats in a quiet road in Maida Vale. At nine o'clock on the previous Friday evening, 15th June, he had left the block and started out across the road, where he had been knocked over and killed by a vehicle travelling at considerable speed.

There had been no witness of the accident, though people in other flats had heard the impact. By the time they looked out of their windows, only parked cars were visible.

Rod Tisdale had lived alone, and had apparently spent the day in his flat working. Investigations so far suggested that he had not spoken to anyone on the telephone except for his agent, and had not then mentioned any plans to go out. There was nothing in his diary to indicate why he set out at nine o'clock. He might have been walking towards Maida Vale tube station. He might have been going to the local pub (though he was very rarely seen in there). He might just have been going out for a walk.

Police investigations would continue to try to track down the errant vehicle which had killed him, so an adjournment was requested. The coroner granted it in a voice that did not expect much more to be discovered and commented on the alarming increase in hit and run accidents.

There was no one Charles Paris recognised at the inquest, so he left little the wiser. The death could just have been an accident. On the other hand, if the potential murderer were someone Rod Tisdale knew, the murder would have been fairly easy to set up. He had only to ring the writer, fix a meeting-place which would involve his crossing the road, and sit and wait for him to come out.

So, just another death, and apparently an accidental one. Every attempt at a pattern Charles started was soon frustrated. He had been on very promising lines with Bernard Walton cast as villain, but that approach had been ruined by the latest incident. Rod Tisdale's death would do nothing to halt the progress of *The Strutters*, and was,

93

on the contrary, a positive loss to Bernard, who had looked to the writer to come up with a new star vehicle for him.

So, even if Bernard Walton hadn't got the one alibi Charles could never crack, his motivation was gone, and, with it, fantasies of the star bringing in hired killers to do his dirty deeds.

Charles tried to contact Bernard a few days later with a view to checking a few facts about Scott Newton's death, but the housekeeper said Mr Walton had gone for a month's holiday to his villa in Sardinia. Since this was supported the next day by a photograph of the star beaming farewells at Heathrow Airport, there was no reason to disbelieve it. (Charles's first cynical reaction to the news had been that Bernard's Publicity Manager had packed him off to Sardinia in the hope that a well-timed kidnap might bring his client back to public attention.)

So, if any further accidents hit *The Strutters* team during the next month, it was pretty unlikely that Bernard Walton had anything to do with them.

But for the next couple of weeks there was no sign of any sort of accident. Charles began to think that the first three must after all be just unfortunate coincidences.

All that happened was that *The Strutters* continued to be made, and that was quite a tiring process for all concerned. The basic pattern for the first burst of the series had been for Tuesday evening recordings, with a read-through for the next episode the following morning. Six weeks of this was already a heavy schedule, but the need to fit in extra filming days to replace those lost after Scott's death made it very heavy indeed. Saturday rehearsals crept in, then Sunday ones. Even Charles, on whom the demands of fourteen lines and two moves a week were not onerous, began to get tired. The strain on the principals must have been enormous.

George Birkitt reacted by occasional bouts of temperament. He was not used to learning so many lines every week and was often still to be seen with script in hand at the Dress Run on recording day. He got very cross when the poor little Assistant Stage Manager charged with the task prompted him, and kept complaining that he found the lines difficult to remember because they were so badly written.

Aurelia Howarth, on the other hand, always knew her lines after a couple of days and generally showed professionalism and stamina which would have been remarkable in an actress half her age. She still appeared very anxious, no doubt worried about Cocky's health, but did not let this interfere with her work. She lived up to the theatrical standard of a 'trouper' and, by contrast, showed up George Birkitt's relative immaturity.

In spite of her worn looks, she did not seem to have lost any of her enthusiasm for the business. Indeed, a couple of days after Rod Tisdale's death, Charles was amused to hear her asking Peter Lipscombe whether he'd yet read the books she'd lent him. She was sure there was series potential there.

Peter apologised, promised they were next on his list, really. Charles had heard that from too many producers to take it too seriously. Though many television producers can read scripts, it's a very rare one who can manage a whole book.

So there didn't seem much prospect for Aurelia's idea. But Charles was impressed that at her age and in the middle of such a tight schedule she was still on the look-out for a new project.

With all the pressures, a kind of peace and community spirit came over the production. They all spent so much time together that they had to choose between constant arguments or conviviality and fortunately most opted for the latter. Even Charles began to see the advantages of television. It was almost like having a regular job.

The audience reaction to the recordings didn't change much, but everyone seemed quite happy about it, and Charles came to share the indifference to, or even contempt of audiences, which is common to most people who work in television. Bob Tomlinson was all set to come in with his electronic hilarity in the dubbing suite, so it hardly mattered what the people shovelled out of coaches into the studio seats thought of the show. The only function of their reaction was to tell the viewing audience at home where the jokes were intended to be.

Charles also got closer to Jay Lewis. The young PA

95

seemed to have ended her relationship with Nick Coxhill and to be more or less available. She seemed to enjoy Charles's company and, though he got a little sick of the received wisdom of Phil Middleton and Ernie Franklyn Junior, news of the progress of VTR editing and the doings of Jay's flatmate who worked in Film Research, he enjoyed hers. She really was very pretty.

Sometimes Charles wondered if his continuing attraction to girls young enough to be his daughter arose from his incomplete relationship with his real daughter, Juliet. But, since it didn't change facts or get him anywhere, he never indulged such speculation for long.

He didn't make any move with Jay for the time being. They were working too closely together for him to risk a rebuff or any awkwardness. But he made his interest clear, and planned in a vague way for some sort of advance just before the break in recording sequence in mid-July.

Thoughts of crime receded. When he spoke to Gerald Venables after one of the recordings, he said he'd decided there was nothing to be investigated, except for a sequence of coincidences. The only thing that had ever made him think differently was the words of Sadie which he had overheard. And there was no chance of finding out any more about them.

After the recording before the overnight filming, the usual group of cast (including Toby Root, who'd played the part of Colonel Strutter's friend) and camp followers (very camp, in some cases) gathered in the bar for a quick drink, because the week ahead was busy. Readthrough the following morning and rehearsal all day. Then, because of Union regulations covering the Thursday night's shoot, no rehearsal on the Thursday or Friday. Pick up again Saturday morning, rehearse Sunday, somehow be ready for the Crew Run Monday at noon, and into the studio on the Tuesday. It wasn't long to get a half-hour of television together.

With this in mind, neither Dame Aurelia Howarth nor George Birkitt went up for a drink. Both no doubt (though the latter would never admit it) had gone back to do a bit of work on the week's lines.

The absence of his idol left Aurelia's Number One Fan

at something of a loose end. Since his first contested appearance, Romney Kirkstall had come to every recording and hung around on the fringe of Aurelia's cricle in the bar afterwards. He never had a drink, neither buying for himself nor accepting anyone else's offer.

He looked so helpless that once he had got a large Bell's (very skilfully bought by Peter Lipscombe), Charles went across to him.

'Dob not coming up?' asked Romney Kirkstall anxiously.

'Don't think so. Busy schedule this week. I expect she's gone back to catch up on some sleep.'

'Oh dear.' The little man looked very upset. The focus of his whole week had been removed.

'I'm sure she'll come up for a drink next time,' Charles comforted. 'It's just that we've got an overnight shoot on Thursday, so it's a tight week.'

Romney Kirkstall still looked distraught. 'I wanted to see her. I've got a book I wanted her to autograph.'

'Oh. Well, next week.'

'I suppose so,' Romney Kirkstall conceded dismally. 'I was so excited to find it, though. It's a biography of Dob that I've been looking for for ages. Found it on a barrow outside a second-hand bookshop in Putney.'

'Oh, really.'

'It's very rare, you know. Called *I Dream of Dancing*. You know, after the song.'

'Oh yes. I've heard of it.' It was difficult not to have done. The song had been a big hit in a revue in the early Thirties and had virtually become Aurelia Howarth's signature tune.

'Oh, I did want to get her signature today.' Romney Kirkstall still sounded desolated.

'You'll get it in a week.'

'Anything can happen in a week.'

Charles looked up sharply, his dormant detective instinct aroused. But no, there was no threat in Romney Kirkstall's words. He was a little man with an obsession, but that obsession wasn't murder.

Charles thought perhaps showing an interest would cheer him up, so asked Romney if he might look at the book.

It was the right question. There was a scurry into the

duffle bag and the precious trophy was presented to him.

The book was a battered little blue volume. Presumably it had had a decorative dust jacket, but that was long gone. Charles turned instinctively to the date of publication — 1940. It was not surprising that Romney Kirkstall had had difficulty in finding it. Most books vanish pretty quickly, but show business biographies must be the most quickly dated and evanescent forms of literature.

The name of the book's author was Max de Pouray, which meant nothing to Charles. He glanced at the text as he flicked through and recognised the breathless sycopahncy of the genre.

And of course Dob appeared in his famous Midnight Revue at the 'Pav'. All the stars in London's theatrical galaxy were there, and she outshone them all. Dressed in the simplest gown of white silk, in such company as the Prince of Wales, Lord and Lady Louis Mountbatten, Mrs Dudley Ward, the Duchess of Portland, Lady Victoria Wemyss, the Duke and Duchess of Westminster, the Duke of Norfolk and half the noble scions of Debrett's, a glittering company that must have left most of this sceptred isle's stately homes empty, it was Dob who was the 'wow' of the evening . . .

There was a lot more in similar vein, but Charles found the photographs more interesting. They were brownish, and many had the posed quality of publicity stills. What they revealed most forcibly was Aurelia Howarth's natural beauty. At fifteen, while she was a humble member of the chorus, she already had a remarkable purity of line and, maturing through the photographs, she retained the softness of youth. In spite of the vagaries of hair-styling and the ridiculous nature of some of her revue costumes, her quality shone through. And the soft studio lighting of the period gave her outline that blurred indistinction which she somehow still retained.

There were a few less posed shots, though they still looked pretty formal. Over dinner at the Café Royal. In a deck chair on a transatlantic liner. Relaxing on the beach at Nice with a handsome young man . . . It was with shock that Charles realised that her escort must be her husband. A photograph of their wedding confirmed it.

It was hard to imagine from the grinning skeleton he

was that Barton Rivers had once been such a dashing figure. With his body fleshed out and a thick crop of dark hair sleeked back on his head, he looked very much the matinee idol.

But the photographs did not offer much evidence of his career. After all, the book's subject was Aurelia, and it seemed that they had rarely worked together. There was one shot of them with two other couples dancing in front of a backdrop of a desert island. The caption read *'In the Palm of My Hand with a Palm Overhead* from *Careless Feet.'* And there was a picture of the pair sitting in a Bentley over the legend. 'Husband and Wife — from *Death Takes A Short Cut.'* The photograph looked like a film still.

What was remarkable about it was that they looked so familiar. The photograph was only a half-page and the whole of the Bentley was in shot, so it was difficult to see much detail of their faces. Aurelia wore one of her floating gowns, and a hat tied on with a scarf. Barton wore a blazer and cravat, and his hair was obscured by a large white flat cap. The car, which must have been a lot newer when the photograph was taken, was identical to the one they now drove around in.

In fact, to the casual eye, the photograph could have been taken a few weeks before, when the couple drove away from Bernard Walton's house after the day's filming.

'Do you know anything about this film?' Charles asked.

Romney Kirkstall shook his head. 'Never heard of it. But then I've always concentrated on Dob's theatrical work. That is, until she stopped doing theatre and started television.

Charles looked again at the photograph, but was aware of Romney Kirkstall's hands reaching out for the book. 'If you don't mind . . .'

There was a note of paranoia in the little man's voice, as if he were genuinely afraid Charles was going to appropriate his prize.

'Okay, thank you very much for letting me look at it.' He handed the book back and, without another word, Romney Kirkstall stuffed it into his duffle bag and scuttled off.

Jay Lewis was chattering to some other young PAs. She

turned round angrily when he ran a finger down her spine, but softened when she saw who it was. Which was nice.

'Hello, Charles.'

'Hi. I wondered if you fancied coming out for a meal.'

'Now?'

'Uh-huh.'

'I've just fixed to go and eat with Dinky and Lucretia.' She indicated the other girls. 'You could come with us, I suppose.'

'Not really what I had in mind.'

She grinned a grin that suggested she knew what he did have in mind. And didn't object too much.

'Another time, maybe,' he proposed.

'Hock—A.'

'And do you think your flatmate in Film Research could find out something for me?'

'I'm sure she could.'

'Good. I'll tell you about it when we have our meal.'

He got another drink (had to buy his own — Peter Lipscombe had left) and looked round for someone to talk to. Most of the cast had gone. Jay and he friends were collecting their coats by the door. Knots of cameramen still drank lager. Men in lumberjack checked shirts grumbled ominously. Robin Laughton, the hearty Floor Manager, held court to some young men at a low table. Charles drifted over to join them.

Robin seemed pleased to see him. He was showing off his savoir-faire to a group of trainee Floor Managers, and wanted to demonstrate his easy familiarity with the stars. Since there weren't any stars in the bar, he would make do with Charles Paris.

'Charles, just passing on a few wrinkles to the lads here. Charles Paris, this is Bob, and Tony and . . . er . . .'

'Dick,' supplied the youngest man, who looked vaguely familiar. 'Actually, Charles, we met on *The Strutters'* pilot. I was trailing Robin on that.'

'Ah yes.' That would explain the familiarity. 'What've you been doing since?'

'Oh, trailing other stuff. I went and did some of the Wragg and Bowen filming, and then I've been following this series for the elderly. Do you know they've got this presenter on that called Ian Reynolds, who's nearly eighty?'

'Yes, I had heard.'

'He's a great old boy. He's not got a nerve in his body when it comes to —'

Robin Laughton decided that the trainee had held the floor long enough and interrupted. 'I must tell Charles about you and the walkie-talkie.'

'Oh.' Dick did not look keen on having the anecdote repeated.

But Robin Laughton pressed on with enthusiasm. Clearly it was a story that was going to show up Dick's inexperience. 'Charles, you know we all carry round these walkie-talkies, so that we can talk back to production control?'

'Yes.'

'Well, one thing you've got to remember is to switch them off, otherwise you're wired for sound at all times . . .'

'Yes.'

The other two trainee Floor Managers snickered in anticipation of the story they had heard before, and Dick looked even more uncomfortable, but Robin continued inexorably. 'Well, when Dick was very new, two or three months back, he was all wired up and he forgot about it and went off to the Gents to have a shit . . .'

This was the cue for the other trainees to burst into open laughter, which they dutifully did.

'Everyone,' Robin Laughton continued, 'heard everything. You got a round of applause when you came back into the studio, didn't you, Dick?'

'Yes.' He grinned and, reckoning that his baiting was now finished, tried to change the subject. 'What interests me, Charles, about —'

But Robin Laughton wasn't going to let him off the hook that easily. 'Oh, Dick kept doing things like that when he started. After the lavatory incident, he went and lost his set one day . . .'

'Well, I mislaid it.' Dick was not enjoying this crude masculine teasing. 'I just put it down somewhere. There's a lot to think about when you start.'

'Oh yes, a great deal,' Robin Laughton mocked. Charles saw the Floor Manager for what he was, the sort of man who would offer no sympathetic assistance to trainees in his charge, but would take delight in watching them make mistakes. Having started niggling at Dick, he couldn't leave the subject alone. 'Actually, it was on *The Strutters'* pilot you lost it, wasn't it? Lost it for the bloody Dress Run. My, you *were* a useful Floor Manager, weren't you?'

The other trainees laughed obediently. Dick spoke angrily. 'Look, I found it straight after. Right at the beginning of Line-up.'

Robin Laughton continued his mockery. 'He'd left it switched on, needless to say. Relaying anything it picked up into Production Control. Lucky the batteries weren't completely flat.'

'Where had you left it?' asked Charles, suddenly interested.

'In the Quick Change Room.'

'And you found it just after six?'

'Yes.'

'And was there anyone in the Quick Change Room?'

Dick was relieved at the change of interrogator and replied readily. 'Yes. Sadie Wainwright was in there, being her usual bad-tempered self.'

'Bad-tempered to you or to someone else?'

'Both. She appeared to be in the middle of an argument when I went in, and then bit my head off.'

'Who was in there with her?'

'Aurelia Howarth.'

CHAPTER NINE

Rod Tisdale's final message to the world, the sixth (or, if you count the pilot, seventh) episode of *The Strutters*, was on a theme he had used before. In *What'll the Neighbours Say?* much of the comedy had derived from the conflict between the wildly bohemian (if slightly overmature) Bernard Walton character and his more conventional neighbours, the Strutters. In *The Strutters*, the reactionary disapproval of the Colonel and his wife was moved to the centre of the action, and directed at everything in general and at their son in particular. This character, played by Nick Coxhill, became increasingly indistinguishable from the Bernard Walton character in *What'll the Neighbours Say?* He it was now who turned up in episodes with black girlfriends or wearing kaftans (sit coms must be the only places in the world where kaftans are still worn as a symbol of Bohemianism) or playing music too loud. (In the original script for this last plot, Rod Tisdale had gone daringly modern and had the character smoking pot, but West End Television, feeling this was a bit strong, had changed it to playing music too loud, which, as they said, 'made the same point'.)

Having reasserted the basic polarities of his traditional script, Rod Tisdale seemed determined to adapt all his old plots for the new series. But for the unfunny intervention of death, there was little doubt that all of the *What'll the Neighbours Say?* storylines would, in time, have reappeared in the guise of episodes of *The Strutters*. However, it was not to be, and with the appointment of Willy and Sam Tennison, who knew what direction the series would take? (Actually, one could have a pretty good guess. It was only a matter of time before the Nick Coxhill character was supplied with a dizzy wife to exchange darlings with, and Colonel and Mrs Strutter were moved back into subsidiary roles.)

All this preamble is necessary to explain the reason for the night filming that was so disturbing the rehearsal schedule of *The Strutters*. In Episode Six (or, if you count the pilot, Seven) the plot, simplified (but not much) was as follows:

Colonel Strutter and his son argue violently about politics. The Colonel is a true-blue Conservative (jokes about being blue in the face too) and the Nick Coxhill character is a follower of Marx (sequence of jokes about Groucho, Harpo and Chico, which are compulsory in all sit coms which mention Marx). The son, in a kaftan, then meets a friend, also in a kaftan, who has just started a new political party, the Conservation (jokes about recycled paper and brown rice) and Union (brassiere jokes about 'One out, all out') Party. Friend suggests son should bridge the gap between the generations and invite his father to come and speak at the inaugural meeting of the new party. Son rings mother, who takes message and, daffily, mishears 'Conservation and Union Party' as 'Conservative and Unionist Party'. End of Part One. Commercial Break.

Part Two opens with Colonel and Mrs Strutter (on film) in the street, looking for the venue of the meeting and being amazed by the Bohemianism of the people they see going in. (All the extras involved wear kaftans to demonstrate their Bohemianism and have long hair and beards, thus adding considerably to the make-up bill for the episode.) The rest of Part Two is a studio sequence of the actual meeting in which misunderstandings abound, and everyone gets the wrong end of every available stick with, as in all good sit coms, 'hilarious consequences'.

The above plot had appeared in a very early episode of *What'll the Neighbours Say?*, in which Bernard Walton formed a new political party called 'The Brigade of Hard Red Unions', which his father (a character who didn't get on with Bernard and was quickly dropped from the series) misheard as 'The Brigade of Guards Reunion'. With, once again, 'hilarious consequences'.

The only difference between the two was that in *The Strutters* episode, all the other regular characters went along to the meeting to witness the Colonel's discomfiture. Which meant that Reg the golf club barman once again displayed his trousers, and Charles Paris had to turn up to West End Television for a nine p.m. make-up call, before being taken by coach to the condemned road in Clapham which the Location Manager had selected for the night's filming.

All the impedimenta of filming lay ready when the coach arrived. The crew had been booked for the full night and so were guaranteed 'Golden Time' (the best rate of overtime), regardless of when they finished. As a result the men in lumberjack checked shirts hadn't told them to slow down and they had been very efficient.

It was still a warm summer evening and not quite dark. But a fierce glow brighter than daylight came from the terrace of houses which was to be used as the location. Huge lights on tall metal stands were trained on them ready for filming. Cables ran from these to a variety of vans and lorries. Make-up caravans and mobile dressing rooms spread down the street. The double-decker bulk of the location caterers' bus loomed to one side. Extras in beards and kaftans sat around, plotting as ever how to get personally 'directed' by the director, thus raising their status (and fee) to that of 'walk-on'. There could be no doubt that a film crew was around.

So was a large crowd of gawpers. This was inevitable. The paraphernalia always attract an audience, and the clemency of the weather increased their numbers. Many had been standing outside local pubs and followed the film transport with interest. It was not an area where a great deal happened.

There was some raucous shouting from the crowd, but they seemed fairly good-humoured. Robin Laughton, the Floor Manager, walking round with his walkie-talkie, was of the opinion that they would soon disperse once the novelty had worn off and it got later.

The Location Manager, looking a little anxious, said he hoped that was the case. 'There seem to be a lot more people round here than I expected. I thought all the houses were empty. Most of them are boarded up.'

'Squatters, I should think,' said Robin Laughton. 'What time of day did you do your recce?'

'Afternoon. Hardly anyone around then. Just the old couple who live in that house right in the middle. I fixed a fee with them all right.'

'If you get trouble, maybe you'll have to pay some of this lot off.'

The Location Manager nodded uncertainly. It was part of his job to carry round pockets full of fivers to buy off anyone who objected to the filming. 'There are a lot of them, though.'

'They'll soon clear off once they see how boring it is. Don't you worry, my son.'

'Is Bob ready to start filming?'

Robin Laughton shook his head. 'Dob's not here yet.'

'Wasn't she coming in the coach?'

'No, special dispensation, she was to come and get made up here.'

'What, that old looney coming here in the Bentley? He's probably driven her to the wrong place.'

'No, no, we've sent a hire car for her. Old Barton'll be safely tucked up in bed by now.'

George Birkitt, standing by Charles, had overheard the end of this conversation. 'Oh no, it's the bloody limit!'

'What is?'

'Bloody Dob. Coming straight here. Not getting made up at W.E.T. like the rest of us.'

'Oh, come on. She's tired. Needs as much rest as she can get.'

'Don't you think I'm bloody tired?'

'I'm sure you are, but you're not seventy-five.'

'Huh. It's all very well, everyone kow-towing to her all the time, but who's carrying this bloody show, that's what I want to know. I mean, really, I'm the one who has to keep the thing going. I carry the story-line every bloody week, while she just twitters around charmingly. And yet who gets the top billing? Huh. You know I'm not the sort of person to fuss over details, but I think that billing'll have to be looked at on the next series.'

Aurelia arrived soon, clutching Cocky's basket, full of apologies for being late. The minicab driver, like all mini-cab drivers, hadn't known the way and had got lost. But she wouldn't be a minute honestly, darling. And she hurried into the make-up caravan.

Charles strolled over to the lit area and leant against one of the tall light-stands. ''Ere, keep off that. Not stable,' said the voice of one of the men in lumberjack checked shirts.

Charles moved away and looked at the stand. It was perfectly stable, in fact, mounted on a wheeled tripod. Metal locks were fixed down on the wheels to prevent it from slipping down the incline of the street. Still, television is full of people telling you not to touch this or that. Charles didn't want to precipitate a demarcation dispute by arguing.

Rather than getting smaller, the crowd of sightseers had increased. He looked at his watch. Of course, pubs just closed. The thought made him feel in his pocket, where his hand met the reassuring contour of a half-bottle of Bell's. Essential supplies for a night's filming.

There was irony in the scene before him. Here was a television crew setting out to film television's idea of an

106

Alternative Society scene, and being watched by genuine members of the Alternative Society. It wasn't just their make-up which distinguished the television extras from the people they were meant to represent. Even those who weren't wearing kaftans looked far too groomed, far too designed. Television, particularly colour television, is a glamorising medium and it is very bad at reproducing authentic shoddiness.

But there was no doubt that the crowd of spectators was authentically shoddy. They were dusty and poor and bored. The interest the filming was arousing suggested that nothing else much happened in their lives. Probably a lot of them were unemployed. And, as their numbers grew, their good humour seemed to diminish.

Charles heard another whispered consultation between the Floor Manager and the Locations Manager.

'You have cleared the filming with the police, haven't you?'

'Of course I have. First thing I always do.'

'Oh well, if they don't disperse once we start filming, we can get the cops to move them on.'

'I thought you were the one, Robin, who said they'd all disperse without any bother.'

'There weren't so many of them then.'

'Hmm.'

'Well, I think if you slip the noisiest ones a fiver, you'll be all right.'

'I might try it. See how things go.'

Bob Tomlinson bustled up to Robin Laughton. 'Come on, where are the bloody artists? We don't want to fart around all night, for God's sake.'

'I think Dob's nearly ready.'

'Then get her out here. And George. And the others. Come on, if we move, we can knock this lot off in an hour.'

But progress did not prove to be so fast. The artists were assembled and their first set-up, a walk along the road looking at house numbers, was rehearsed. The actors spoke their lines, and the director was satisfied.

'Okay. Let's go for a take.' There was silence. The clapper-board was duly filmed and the item identified verbally by the Floor Manager. 'And — Action!'

But the cast weren't the only people who took the cue. As soon as the word was spoken, the crowd behind the camera started up their noise again, shouting and baying, chanting in unison.

Bob Tomlinson tried again. Again there was silence while the shot was set up. Again, as soon as he cued the actors, the crowd started up. 'Talk to them, Robin,' he said tersely.

Robin Laughton went across towards the crowd in his most jovial Floor Manager manner. He spread his arms wide for attention. 'Listen, everyone, could we have a bit of hush while we're working? We're in a filming situation for a series called *The Strutters,* which you'll be able to see on your telly screens in the autumn. It's going to be a jolly funny show and I'm sure you'll all enjoy it. So we'd be really grateful if you could give us a bit of hush while we're doing our filming. Okay?'

'Why?' asked a tall black youth in a Bob Marley T-shirt.

'Why?' echoed Robin Laughton.

'Yes, why? Why should we let you disrupt our lives just for some tatty television show?'

Robin was baffled. It was a question that had never occurred to him, so he had never considered the answer to it.

The black youth spoke very fluently. He was obviously well educated and not randomly obstructive. He was making a political point. What was more, the rest of the crowd listened to him. He was their leader and they did what he said. The disruption seemed to be an organised protest.

Robin Laughton, unable to provide any sort of answer to the black youth's question, wandered back to Bob Tomlinson and beckoned the Location Manager across. They conferred.

Then the Location Manager went across to the crowd. The black youth had his back turned and was talking to a group of other young men. The Location Manager joined the group and appeared to make some suggestion.

Suddenly the black youth leapt in the air, waving a piece of paper in his hand. 'Hey, look, man — five pounds. You ever see one like that, man? Come on, everybody, this man's giving away five pound notes. Make sure you all get one.'

'No, no,' protested the unfortunate Locations Manager. 'I haven't got enough for everyone. I just wanted to persuade everyone that —'

'What is it — bribery now?' The black youth was suddenly very quiet. 'Oh yes, money buy off everything, eh? Well, listen, man, why should we put up with you coming round here? What you say it is — comedy show? So you think the way we live's funny, eh?'

'No, not at all. We just want to get on with our work. Look, you wouldn't like it if we came along and interfered with your work now, would you?'

This proved an unfortunate thing to say. 'Our work, is it? Sorry, brother, we don't have any work. That's why we live here, you know. That's why we live in these houses. That's why we don't like you making fun of our houses.'

The Location Manager was beginning to lose his temper. 'But they're not your houses. You're only bloody squatters.'

'And why are we squatters, man? We're squatters because this lousy government don't build no houses. We're squatters because this government don't care about anything except making the rich richer.'

Hearing the political turn of the conversation, Bob Tomlinson decided to join in with his common touch. 'Listen, mate, I'm with you. I vote Labour, just like you do. I don't want this lot in. But they're here and all we have to do is make the best of it. And all I want to do right now is get the work I got to do done, and get into bed for a good night's sleep. So what do you say? You give us no bother and we'll give you no bother.'

He chuckled disarmingly, but didn't persuade his audience. 'What do you mean?' asked the black youth. 'You don't give us any bother, huh? You take over the whole bloody street, and half the side streets off it. You fill the whole place with your bloody vans and buses and your big cars — all your bloody BMWs and Rovers and Bentleys and Daimlers and Mercs — and you say you don't give us no bother. Why should we be put out by you fat cats, eh?'

The Location Manager nodded to Bob Tomlinson and walked away. 'Now listen, son,' said the director in a new, hard voice. 'He's gone to phone for the police. We have police permission to be here, you know, and if they come along, I think you'd be wise to be out of sight.'

'Oh, I see, it's threats now, is it? What d'you think we care about the bloody pigs. Okay, so you've got police permission. Big deal. Did you ever ask our permission? Eh?'

'We got permission from the couple in that house over there, who, as I understand it, are the only people with a legal right to live here.'

'What do you know about legal rights?'

'I know who deserves them.'

'What do you mean by that?'

'I mean I know the difference between someone who works for a living and someone who just scrounges on the state.'

'Hey, who you calling a scrounger, man?'

'You know bloody well who I'm calling a scrounger.'

'You want a punch in the mouth?'

'Why, do you?'

Slap on his cue, at this moment Peter Lipscombe appeared beaming through the crowd. 'I say, is everything okay?'

His appearance did at least avert the incipient fight between Bob Tomlinson and his antagonist, but it didn't bring the start of filming any nearer. He tried to explain the complex costs of filming to the crowd, but they didn't seem susceptible to budgetary arguments.

The actors were still standing round in the lit area, ready to resume work if required, but eventually Robin Laughton came across and suggested they should go into the caravans until the atmosphere settled a bit.

Charles found himself in the make-up caravan with Aurelia Howarth. The actress busied herself with Cocky in his little basket.

'Quite frightening, all those people, aren't they?' he observed.

She shrugged. 'I suppose so. It reminds me of entertaining the troops during the War. You got that same feeling of the power of a crowd.'

'And you don't find that frightening?'

'Not really, darling.' She sounded genuinely uncon-
cerned, though a note of anxiety came into her voice as
she turned back to the dog. 'How's my little boy then?'

'Do you think we'll get anything done tonight?'

'Oh yes, surely, darling. They'll get bored and go away.'

The noise had certainly died down. Charles looked
through the caravan window. The crowd was dwindling.

'Yes, they've made their point. And if the police do
come . . .'

'I think it would be as well if the police didn't come,'
Dame Aurelia Howarth observed shrewdly. 'That might
just antagonise them further.' But her attention was
elsewhere. 'How's my little Cocky then?'

'Is he okay?' Better show an interest.

'He's not a well boy.'

'He means a lot to you.'

'Of course. If anyone hurt Cocky, I'd . . .' She looked
at Charles very straight and he felt the daunting power of
those famous eyes. When she continued, her voice was very
quiet, but very determined. 'I'd kill them.'

Everything fell into place. As well as determination,
there was obsession in the eyes. On three occasions Aurelia
Howarth had had the opportunity. She had been definitely
identified as the one who had threatened Sadie Wainwright.
The PA had certainly spoken dismissively of Cocky. Was
it not likely that Scott Newton and Rod Tisdale had done
the same? Or was he back to his earlier blackmailing
theory? Had Scott Newton witnessed Sadie's death
and . . . ?

Well, if there had to be a confrontation, there was no
time like the present. Charles took a deep breath. 'Aurelia,
when Sadie Wainwright died —'

But before he could say more, they were disturbed by a
sudden shout of anger from outside. The crowd had
once again erupted in fury. Charles and Aurelia rushed to
the door of the caravan to see the cause.

It was the location caterers. Oblivious to the commotion,
they had started to lay out a lavish selection of salads and
meats and wines on trestle tables outside their bus. A
section of the crowd had seen this and, infuriated by the
ostentation, screamed for the others to join them as they

111

rushed forward.

The horde descended, seizing plates and bowls and throwing them to the ground. When the film crew tried to intervene, they had food hurled at them. Within seconds, everyone was involved in a bizarre fight outside the location caterers' bus.

Terrines of pâté cracked against skulls, rare beef slices slapped in faces, glazed chicken wings rediscovered flight, strawberries spattered, mayonnaise flowed down denim shoulders, coleslaw matted into layered hair.

How the fight would have developed was impossible to say. An awful thud and a scream froze the action and drew everyone's attention back to the lit area.

In the middle of it lay the still body of Robin Laughton, pinned beneath the metal mass of a toppled light.

'Oh no.' Aurelia Howarth's face had lost all its colour. 'Not another death. Oh, my God, no!'

But there was no doubt that the Floor Manager was in a death situation.

CHAPTER TEN

Since they had already been summoned to move on the crowd of spectators, the police were on the scene of the death quickly. They took charge and were very efficient. Technicians and actors were asked to wait in the caravans until the police were ready to take statements from them. The crowd who had disrupted the filming seemed to have melted away. They would have stayed and argued their rights with the police over the filming, and enjoyed the exercise; but now there was a death to be investigated they made themselves scarce.

Two plain-clothes detective-sergeants were taking the statements. The one Charles got looked bored and seemed keen to get the basic questions over as quickly as possible. 'You see anything unusual?'

'Well, the whole scene was fairly unusual. With the fight going on, food flying in every direction . . .'

'Yes, I know all that. I mean, anything unusual near the

112

light that fell and killed Mister . . .' He consulted notes.
'. . . Laughton.'

'No, but I did notice that the wheels of the light were firmly locked earlier.'

'Yes. What I'm really asking is did you see anyone tamper with the light-stand. I gather the crowd was trying to break up your filming, so I suppose we can't rule out the possibility of sabotage. Did you see anyone go near the lights?'

'No, but everything was such chaos that —'

'Yes, Mr Paris. At the time of the fight, did you see where John Odange was?'

'Who's John Odange?'

'He's the black guy who was apparently leading the crowd.'

'Oh yes. I saw him by the food. I remember, because he emptied a lemon meringue pie over our producer, Peter Lipscombe.' Charles couldn't help smiling. The image was one that would stay with him and bring comfort in his old age.

'So you didn't see Odange go near the lights?'

'No.'

'Hmm.' The detective-sergeant sounded disappointed. 'We've had trouble with him before.'

It seemed that the black youth's view that society was conspiring against him may have had some justification. 'No,' said Charles firmly. 'He was right at the centre of the crowd all the time. If he had tampered with the lights, everyone would have seen.'

The detective-sergeant nodded in a bored way. 'We'll have to pull him in and talk to him anyway. Okay, Mr Paris, if you could ask the next member of the cast to —'

'There is one thing,' said Charles. There was no point in keeping all his suspicions to himself. After all, it was the police's job to investigate crime and they were much better qualified to do it than he was.

'Yes?' There wasn't a lot of interest in the word.

'Of course this death could just have been an unfortunate accident . . .'

'That's rather the way it looks, Mr Paris. Unless we can get any evidence to the contrary.'

'The only thing is . . . it's not the first accident that's happened on this show. First there was a PA who —'

'Yes, yes, Mr Paris, thank you. I'm well aware of all that. Every one of your colleagues who I've talked to has mentioned the sequence of accidents, and I'm sure it's been very worrying for you. Maybe someone quoted *Macbeth* in a dressing room or something.'

The detective-sergeant spoke as to a tiresome child. It was something Charles had got used to through his career. For a lot of people, actors would always remain a self-dramatising and infantile breed.

He kept his temper. 'Okay, it may sound fanciful. All I'm saying is that, if you are thinking of sabotage, then it need not have been perpetrated by someone in the crowd; it could have been someone connected with the production.'

'Thank you very much for your invaluable advice, Mr Paris. Yes, I admit it does sound a little fanciful, but we will certainly bear every possibility in mind in our investigations. I can assure you that we are already aware of the coincidence of accidents which have surrounded your precious production, and if there is any link between them, you can rely on us to find it. Now, if you will allow me to get on . . .'

Charles wasn't sure. Maybe the police had got the show under surveillance, maybe they had followed all his reasoning through step by step, maybe they were way ahead of him and just waiting to make an arrest. All he knew was that it would be a long time before he shared his suspicions with the police again. Their opinion of amateur detectives was all too clear.

Outside in the street, where the apparatus of filming had mostly been cleared up, he met Jay Lewis, looking young and waif-like in the moonlight.

'Have you been through the grilling too?'

She nodded. 'Not very nice. Poor Robin.'

'Has Aurelia gone?'

'Yes. I organised a car for her about an hour ago. She looked exhausted. I'm just waiting for mine to come.'

'Ah.'

'Actually, Charles, you're Bayswaterish, aren't you?

114

I'm Notting Hill. You could share the cab.'

'Great. If you're sure that's okay . . .'

She was. In the cab she still seemed waif-like, so it was only kind for him to put his arm round her. On the journey, with the predictable interruptions to give directions to the driver, who appeared never to have driven in London before, a degree of intimacy was established.

They arrived outside her flat first. She didn't seem keen to leave him. 'My flat-mate's away. I don't really like to go in on my own. After what happened to Robin . . .'

Charles, ever the obliging gentleman, dismissed the cab. As they climbed up the stairs, he said, 'About your flat-mate, you know I said I wanted to pick her brains on Film Research . . .'

'Oh yes.'

'I wonder if you'd mind asking her about a movie Aurelia did with her husband. Late Thirties, I should think. Called *Death Takes a Short Cut.*'

'I've never heard of it.'

'Nor have I, sweetie. That's why I'm asking.'

'Hock-A. I'll ask her.'

Jay Lewis opened the door of her flat. Once she had closed it, she came into Charles's arms.

In bed he disentangled himself lazily. 'Very nice indeed.'

'Really. You mean it?'

'Certainly do.'

She sighed. 'There's so much to learn.'

'As a PA?'

'Yes, and . . .'

'And sex?'

'Uh-huh.'

'Well, I think you have a natural aptitude for it.'

'Good.' She snuggled into his shoulder. 'You know, Ernie Franklyn Junior says a PA should really be prepared to sleep with anyone.'

'Oh does he?' said Charles Paris. 'Thank you very much.'

West End Television Ltd,
W.E.T. House,
235—9 Lisson Avenue,
London NW1 3PQ.
6th July, 1979.

Dear Charles,

I enclose some revised pages for the beginning of Part Two of this week's script. As we lost last night's filming and are working so close to time, Bob and I have decided it'll be simpler to do a rewrite and replace the exterior scene with a new scene in the hall. I turned to Willy and Sam who, at incredibly short notice, have come up with the enclosed, which I think is terrific and well up to the standard of the other scripts I'm getting from them for later episodes. I think we really are on to a very exciting series!

On a slightly sadder note, I heard this morning that Dob's little dog, Cocky, died during the night. As you know, she doted on him and is bound to be very upset. I'm sending this letter to you by taxi to ensure that you get it before going to rehearsal on Saturday. Do be gentle with Dob.

Once again, many thanks for all your hard work on the series. See you at the Crew Run on Monday.

With the warmest good wishes,

Yours sincerely,

Peter

PETER LIPSCOMBE
Producer *The Strutters*

The detective part of Charles's mind was in confusion. Every time he got near a theory which linked the deaths around *The Strutters*, something new came along to break it up. On the Thursday night he had been convinced that Dame Aurelia Howarth had arranged the murders of Sadie Wainwright, Scott Newton and Rod Tisdale, because she had gone slightly dotty and was convinced that they all meant harm to her precious little dog.

But, even as he had reached that conclusion, another death had occurred, a death in which Aurelia could not possibly have had any hand. He was getting rather sick of providing alibis for his main suspects.

And now, to add to the confusion, Cocky had died. So any motivation the dog might have provided for Aurelia was gone. If any more deaths happened, there would have to be another reason for them. Just as there had to be another reason for Robin Laughton's death.

Again Charles was struck by the random nature of all the deaths, except for Rod Tisdale's. If anyone did unlock the wheels of the huge light and push it over, they can't have had Robin Laughton as a specific target. There was no guarantee that the Floor Manager would be standing in the right place at the right time (or, from his own point of view, the wrong place at the wrong time). Like Scott Newton's death, the latest accident seemed a random act of sabotage. There was no guarantee that the light would hit anyone, and certainly no guarantee that it would kill anyone it did hit.

So he was back to indiscriminate violence against the whole series. And the only person to whom he could attribute a motive for that was currently sunning himself in Sardinia and maybe waiting for a well-publicised kidnap.

Maybe it was all just coincidence, after all. Maybe, as the condescending detective-sergeant had said, someone had quoted from *Macbeth* in the dressing room, and *The Strutters* was just a bad luck show.

And yet he felt he was missing something. There was something he had heard recently that was important, something that he should have been able to relate to the sequence of deaths. But he couldn't for the life of him remember what it was.

The final recording of the first batch of *The Strutters* on 17th July went well. The cast was relaxed and the tested old formula of the *What'll the Neighbours Say?* script about the political meeting pleased the studio audience.

'Rod Tisdale — what a great writer!' Peter Lipscombe was heard to observe in the bar between buying drinks for people. 'What a terrific talent! Tonight's episode just said it all — still experimenting, never content, always looking for new avenues in the comedic field. What a loss he'll be. You know, I reckon, if someone brought out a book of his scripts, he'd really get the recognition he deserves. He'd be up there with the Sheridans and the Wildes and the

Shaws, no question. But of course no publisher would ever do it, no publisher would have the imagination to do it.'

Willy and Sam Tennison, the archpriest and priestess of the arch, were also there, and, while agreeing absolutely, but absolutely with what Peter said about Rod, who really had been a terrific writer and such a good chum, they had been delighted with the way their little scene had gone, promised well for the future, didn't it, darling, oh yes, darling, really promising, darling, whole show going to be such fun, wasn't it, darling, yes, darling . . .

The cast was animated, too. They were lifted by the audience's reception of the show, but, more than that, they had the prospect of a couple of weeks' rest after the hectic pace of the recent schedule. In fact, given extra filming days and an early readthrough, the break was only going to be nine days, but that was better than nothing and they were all looking forward to it.

George Birkitt put his complaints to one side and, with the prospect of no new lines to forget for a few days, was jovially expansive. Even Dob Howarth seemed to be bearing up pretty well after her loss. She and the grinning Barton stood in the bar like royalty, accepting the servile tributes of its inmates.

Only once did her gracious exterior crack and emotion threaten. Romney Kirkstall was there, as ever, and eventually engaged the attention of his idol. 'Dob,' he said, 'I was terribly upset to hear what happened.'

'Thank you.' She inclined her head and very deliberately changed the subject. 'It'll be good to have a few days' rest. Imagine the luxury of the occasional breakfast in bed . . .'

But her fan persisted. 'Cocky meant a lot to me as well as to you. Anyone who's important to you is important to those of us who hold you dear.'

'Thank you.' She was polite, but wanted the subject dropped.

'So I've made you a small tribute.' Romney Kirkstall reached into his duffle bag and produced a large cross, made from silver cardboard and decorated with sprays of silver tinsel. In the centre of it was a colour photograph of Cocky under a fur-clad arm, cut out of some magazine.

'It says on it,' Romney Kirkstall continued inexorably, ' "To Cocky, for many years a dear friend and companion" '

Tears glistened in Aurelia's huge blurred blue eyes. 'Yes, darling, it's very sweet of you, but —'

'And I've written a poem that goes with it. I do occasionally write poems,' Romney Kirkstall admitted modestly. 'It goes:

Ah, Cocky, though you're far away,
I dream of dancing with you still.
Instead of a Good Boy chocolate drop,
How sad you ate death's bitter pill.

A deep sob broke Aurelia's customary self-restraint, but her fan did not seem to notice the effect his tribute was having. 'I hope you noticed I got in the reference to *I Dream of Dancing*. I was rather pleased with that. And I remembered that Cocky used to like those Good Boy chocolate drops.'

'Yes,' Aurelia managed to say, but she was suffering intensely. 'Barton,' she hissed, 'get rid of him.'

The angular blazered skeleton moved forward with surprising speed and took a firm hold on Kirkstall's sports-jacketed arm. 'Look here, old boy,' he said with a ghastly grin as he steered the fan away, 'little lady's a bit upset. Want to talk to you about the team the selectors are putting up for the Oval. A bit rummy, to my way of thinking.'

The language was still bizarre and dislocated, but the actions were very positive. When it came to defending his wife, Barton Rivers was a daunting figure.

Charles Paris was left with Aurelia.

'I'm sorry,' she said, dabbing at her eyes with a lace handkerchief. 'It's just it's so recent. I had managed to put the poor darling out of my mind, and then to have him going on and on about it . . . He's a dear boy, but . . .'

'I understand. Can I get you a drink or . . .'

'No, I'll be fine in a second. I just . . .' She sobbed again.

The gentlemanly thing to do would have been to start a new inoffensive subject, but Charles couldn't leave the little dog's death yet. Romney Kirkstall's inept rhyme had started a new train of thought. Suppose Cocky's death had been another in the sequence of apparent accidents . . . Suppose he had been poisoned by someone who wanted to get at Aurelia . . . It opened up a whole new range of motivations.

'Dob,' he began. He used the pet name to increase their intimacy. 'Dob, we are all very upset to hear about Cocky's death . . .'

'Thank you, darling. I just want to forget about it, please.'

'Of course.' He'd have to be direct. 'I'm sorry, I have to ask. Did you think there was anything strange about it?'

'Strange?'

'You don't think he could have been poisoned?'

Shock registered on her face, but very swiftly understanding followed. 'I see what you mean, darling. Another of these unfortunate . . . *évènements* . . . ?'

Charles nodded.

'No, darling. He was just a very sick boy. The vet had said he hadn't long. No, he just . . . slipped away in the night.' A sob broke her voice.

'I'm sorry. I had to ask.'

'Of course. I understand.' She took his hand between both of hers. 'And I do appreciate what you're doing for us. There have been too many deaths. They must stop. I'm sure they're just accidents, but, if there is a sequence, if there is a solution, then I'm sure you're the one to find it.'

And she gave him the full beam of those wonderful eyes.

Charles reeled. He was flattered that she seemed to know about his hobby of detection, but he felt much more than that. He felt inspired by her confidence. Here now was a lady in whose honour to pursue his knightly quest. He understood more than ever before why princes had courted her, and young men toasted her, why husbands had dreamed of her while they made love to their wives, and why young soldiers had marched to their deaths with her image imprinted on their minds.

He returned the pressure of her hand. From now on he was determined to solve the accumulating mysteries. For her.

She and her husband left soon after and Charles went across to comfort Romney Kirkstall, who stood forlorn in the bar, drinkless as ever, his duffle bag dangling ineffectually from his hand.

'Do you think she didn't like it?'

'I think it was just the wrong moment, that's all. It

made her think about the dog too much.'

'Mmm. I mean, I have done her things before. You know, cards and so on. And poems too. She's always liked them before.'

'And I'm sure she'd have liked this one, but it was just too soon after the event.'

He mulled that over. 'Yes, I suppose so. I could post it to her.'

'I'd leave it a week or two, if I were you.'

'Yes.'

The little man seemed downcast, so Charles tried to make conversation. 'What do you do, Romney?'

'Do? I collect stuff about Dob.'

'Yes, I know that, but what job do you do?'

'I don't have a job. I came into a bit of money when my mother died, so I gave up my job. I just do the collection now.'

'Oh, I see. And are you going to use all the material to write a book about her?'

'Oh, no, I couldn't write a book. It's just an interest, you know,' Romney Kirkstall replied in a voice which suggested that the only thing strange about the conversation was Charles's need to ask the question.

'So you spend your days collecting?'

'Yes, looking around for stuff a lot of the time. I'm a lot younger than her, you see, I'm only forty-three, so I wasn't around to collect programmes and things at the time. But I go around junk stalls and book shops. It's an interest,' he repeated.

Only forty-three. Charles was surprised. Romney Kirkstall could have been any age, but forty-three seemed very young to have developed this kind of obsession. Maybe, Charles reflected, it was a sign of his own age. When the loonies start looking young . . .

'Actually,' Romney Kirkstall continued, 'I thought of you today.'

'Oh?'

'I was looking for some stuff in a bookshop in the Charing Cross Road — a place Barton Rivers recommended to me, actually — and I came across that book you were talking about.'

'What book?'

121

'Well, you were talking about the film, but it had the same title. *Death Takes A Short Cut*.'

'Oh yes?'

'They'd got a copy of it there. I looked at it, but it hadn't got anything to do with Dob, so I put it back. But, since you asked about it, I thought you might be interested.'

'I am. Thank you. Who was the author?'

'R.Q. Wilberforce. Didn't mean anything to me. You heard of him?'

Charles grimaced. 'It's vaguely familiar. Think he could have been one of those Thirties detective story writers, like E.R. Punshon or Freeman Wills Croft.'

'Never heard of them either,' confessed Romney Kirkstall.

'Well, if you could give me the name of the bookshop . . .'

Romney supplied it. 'I must go,' he said. Then he hesitated, as if to impart some vital piece of information. 'Do you know why I was called Romney?' he asked.

'No.'

'My mother named me after Romney Brent. Friend of Noël Coward's.'

'Ah.'

'Yes.' Romney Kirkstall turned tail and scuttered out.

Jay Lewis was still in the bar and seemed to be looking his way. He sidled up to her and whispered, 'What does Ernie Franklyn Junior say about PAs sleeping with the same person twice?'

'Oh, he says that's all right. He says it's inevitable that relationships develop.'

'Oh, does he? That's very nice of him.'

Charles thought he would like to meet Ernie Franklyn Junior one day, and smash his teeth in. Or perhaps set a posse of indignant PAs on him, to revenge his unflattering generalisations. Charles's previous experience of PAs had taught him (by the unquestionable empirical method of trying to get off with them) that their inclination towards promiscuity was no greater than that of other women. They weren't all as gullible as Jay Lewis.

But he couldn't really complain, as he seemed currently to be a beneficiary of the Ernie Franklyn Junior teaching.

He was in no position to argue.

Nor, for the first hour after they got back to Jay's flat, was he in a position to think much either. But he was in some nice positions that didn't involve too much thinking.

There came a lull and they lay back on the pillows.

'You're just using me for experience, aren't you, Jay?'

'Yes. Ernie Fr—'

'Sure, sure.'

'you don't mind, do you?'

'Why should I mind?'

'you know,' she said slowly, 'I may be coming off *The Strutters*.'

'Oh yes.'

'They need an extra PA on Wragg and Bowen.'

'Ah.'

'I'll see if I can get it. Learn more on a big variety show.'

They turned the light out and dozed.

'Oh, by the way . . .' Jay said suddenly.

'Hmm.'

'I did ask my flatmate about that film you mentioned and she found out about it.'

'What did she find out?'

Was this going to be important? Was this going to be the key that unlocked the Chinese box of mysteries?

Apparently not.

'It never got made,' said Jay.

'Oh.'

'No, it was all set up in 1939. They started, did a couple of days' filming, then war was declared and the whole production was cancelled.'

'Ah,' said Charles Paris, and went to sleep.

CHAPTER ELEVEN

West End Television Ltd,
W.E.T. House,
235—9 Lisson Avenue,
London NW1 3PQ.
18th July, 1979.

Dear Charles,

Just a quick note to say how super last night's show was and to thank you for all the hard work you're putting into this very exciting series.

A few days rest now, which I'm sure you'll be glad of, and then . . . on with the fun! We've got some smashing scripts from Willy and Sam and I think the series is going to go all the way to the top of the ratings!

Look forward to seeing you at the next readthrough on Friday, 27th July.

With the warmest good wishes,

Yours sincerely,

Peter

PETER LIPSCOMBE
Producer *The Strutters*

Good God, did the man never stop writing notes, Charles wondered. Where did he get the time? On the other hand, of course, he was a television producer and there must be a limit to the hours in the day you can spend buying people drinks.

The only other mail he had that day was something offering him a piece of leatherette if he applied for an American Express card and a photocopied sheet from the Red Theatre Co-operative, demanding workers' solidarity against the Right Wing Fascist take-over of Equity. He put these two, together with Peter Lipscombe's note, straight into the wastepaper basket, and decided he might go for a stroll down the Charing Cross Road.

The man in the bookshop was desolated, but the book was gone. 'Sold it to a dealer yesterday. Know him well. He's always on the look-out for that sort of stuff. You a collector?'

'Well, not really. I was just interested in that particular book.'

'Oh. 'Cause I could do you a nice 1930 Austin Freeman. *Mr Pottermack's Oversight*, first edition. Or I got a few early Ngaio Marshes. *Died in the Wool*, 1945. And I think I still got a couple of S.S. Van Dines.'

'But no R.Q. Wilberforces?'

'No, sorry, don't get many in. He didn't really do that many, don't think he did any after the War. Maybe he was killed, don't know. I could take your number, if you like, and if I get an R.Q. Wilberforce, give you a buzz.'

'OK. Thanks.' Charles gave his number. 'But don't worry. It isn't important. You say a dealer bought the one you had . . . ?'

'Yes. Of course, if you're really keen. I could put you in touch with him.'

'I would be grateful.'

'Right. I know him well. Comes in here about once a month. His name's Gregory Watts and he lives down in Kew, I think. Here's his number.'

'Thank you very much.'

'And you're sure it's just the R.Q. Wilberforce you're interested in?'

'For the moment, yes.'

''Cause I mean, far be it from me to tell you your business, but if you are starting a collection, you ought to go for a few more in the genre. I mean, there aren't many R.Q. Wilberforces and they're fairly rare, so I reckon you should widen your sights a bit. I mean, I got a nice early American edition of *The Lady in Black*. That was the title of *Trent's Last Case* over there. You know, Bentley.'

With a loud clang, a penny that had been jammed for some days in a slot in Charles' brain, dropped.

'I've got it!' he shouted.

'Have you really?' asked the bookseller, with some surprise at his vehemence. 'Well, that's quite rare. Now that's a very good basis for a collection.'

But he spoke to an empty shop. The potential collector of R.Q. Wilberforce had shot off down the Charing Cross Road.

Charles contemplated making up for the job, but reckoned it was too risky. Part of him wanted to appear in the tramp guise he had worn as Estragon in *Waiting for Godot* at Glasgow ('Never mind Godot, I spent the entire evening waiting for some distinguished acting' — *The Scotsman*). Another part suggested a socially committed researcher, using the earnest Midlands voice he had perfected for some forgotten *Play for Today* ('Tried to fit a quart into a pint pot and drowned the unfortunate actors in the resulting spillage' — *Sunday Times*).

But he rejected both of these. His prospective quarry had seen him before, and Charles knew from experience that disguise in such circumstances could all too easily lead to discovery.

No, he had to go in his own persona, but he had to have a reason to justify his presence. And it had to be something that would disarm the prejudice his appearance was bound to arouse.

His quarry hadn't heard him speak, so he could certainly do something with his voice, which might help. Perhaps he could use the Liverpudlian he'd used in *The Homecoming* at Leatherhead ('I laughed till I left' — *Leatherhead Herald*). Or the non-specific East Anglian he'd developed for a small-time villain in *Z Cars* ('As regular as clockwork and about as interesting' — *Evening Standard*). Or the Midlands one . . .?

But that wasn't really the problem. He could choose a voice when he got there. The difficulty was a reason for his appearance. He thought.

It came in a flash. Of course, nothing is wasted. Everything is meant.

He went through the contents of his wastepaper basket until he came to the photocopied sheet from the Red Theatre Co-operative.

And he studied it hard.

It was strange revisiting the scene of the near-riot and Robin Laughton's death. The weather was benign, early summer sun washing the old frontages of the condemned terrace and giving them a kind of apologetic grandeur, as if they had somehow regained their youth. In the brightness of the sun he wasn't so aware of the boarded windows and padlocked doors, the flaking paint and angry graffiti.

He wasn't sure what a Red Theatre Co-operative member of his age would wear, because he had never met one. In fact he rather wondered whether there were any members of his age; the ones he had come across were all in their twenties and thirties. They were angry young men — no, he mustn't say that, the use of the expression dated him — *committed* young men — that was better — and girls, often with very short hair, tight jeans and leather blousons, who tended to interrupt rehearsals with queries about what the Equity representative intended to do about the rising unemployment figures, or whether Shakespeare was inextricably allied to the capitalist system. Charles had even, briefly, worked with a Red Theatre Co-operative director on a production of *King Lear,* which saw the play as a socialist parable. To justify this reading, the King had to be seen as a symbol of traditional landowning conservatism and the division of his kingdom as a necessary step towards public ownership. As a result, the political sympathies of the audience had to be with Regan and Goneril in their attempts to reduce the power of the traditional hierarchy and impose a socialist state. Cordelia became a symbol of wishy-washy bourgeois uncommitted apathy, and the entrance of Lear with her dead in his arms showed how non-participation was tantamount to alliance with the corruption of capitalism. The tragedy of the play was the deaths of Cornwall, Regan and Goneril, martyrs to the cause of progress, but the production ended on a note of hope. Albany's lines in the final scene,

> All friends shall taste
> The wages of their virtue, and all foes
> The cup of their deservings,

were transposed to the very end of the play, and signified the start of the revolution. They were greeted by a great shout from all the company, dead bodies included, who all sang 'The Red Flag'. The production, in spite of being hailed by *Time Out* as a 'milestone in political theatre, showing that traditional plays need not just be commercial bullshit', played to small houses throughout its short run.

The same director's productions of *Othello* (about a black school-leaver unable to get a job) and *Macbeth* (an interpretation based on the lines

> No, this my hand will rather
> The multitudinous seas incarnadine,
> Making the green one red)

also failed to reach more than a minority audience.

Given the lack of middle-aged models for his chosen role, Charles wore his own clothes. He went first to the house which had been cleared for filming, and summoned the elderly couple who lived there to the door.

'Hello. My name's Charles Paris. I was involved in the filming that West End Television was doing here the other week.'

'Oh yes.' The old man did not look unwelcoming. 'I wondered when you lot would be back.'

'Oh.'

'I said to Rita, they're bound to be back, didn't I, Rita?'

'You did, Lionel.'

'Why?'

'Well, the way I saw it was, you didn't get no filming done that night, did you? So I put two and two together and realised that you'd want to do it another night, because you need it for your show.'

'No, in fact —'

'And before you say anything else, let me say that I'm going to want twice the money you paid last time. The disruption and noise was much more than what you said it would be.'

It took Charles some time to explain that the filming had been covered in the studio and there wouldn't be another fat facility fee going into the old couple's coffers. Once he understood this, the old man was less accommodating. 'What the bleeding hell d'you want then?'

'I'm looking for someone who was around on the night of the filming. The black youth called John Odange. I wondered if you knew where I might find him.'

'I don't know nothing about that scum! We're respectable people. We got a right to live in this house. We ain't going to move on till the council comes up with what we think's proper accommodation. Are we, Rita?'

'No, Lionel.'

'We're quiet, respectable people,' the old man shouted.

'This used to be a nice road. Now we've got all these bloody squatters, living ten to a house, drinking, taking drugs, playing music! Bloody foreigners, and all! They aren't even house-trained, a lot of them. They're all . . .'

He continued in the same vein for some time. Under this splenetic fusillade, Charles retreated and went to ask someone else where he might find John Odange.

He knocked on one of the doors from which the council's padlock had been unscrewed and was answered by a pretty and very clean young mum with a baby. Yes, John Odange lived three houses down. She didn't know whether he was likely to be in, but it was worth trying.

He was in. His tall frame filled the doorway. He wore a faded mauve T-shirt and black jeans. There was no sign of recognition when he asked what he could do for Charles.

He sounded wary, but not, as Charles had expected, deliberately aggressive.

'I was involved in that filming which West End Television was doing a couple of weeks back.'

'Uh-huh.' Still no overt hostility.

'I was one of the actors in the show and I . . . I wanted to talk about it.' To his annoyance, Charles found he was speaking in his own voice. Also he had difficulty in getting round to his prepared speeches about actors being workers as much as anyone else and the need for education and the vital role of the entertainer in spreading the Marxist message. He was daunted by John Odange, not by the man's size and vouched militancy, but by the sharp intelligence in his eyes. He was not going to be easy to fool.

'Come in.' The tall youth moved to one side and Charles went into the house. Inside it was spotless. The old man up the road wouldn't have believed how clean and sweet-smelling it was.

John Odange indicated a room to the right. It was a bed-sitter lined with books. It too was immaculately tidy. By the window was a desk piled with more books and files. A portable electric typewriter still hummed, suggesting Charles had interrupted composition.

'Are you a writer?' he asked.

The black youth shook his head. 'Only incidentally. I'm a student really. An unaffiliated student.'

'What does that mean?'

'It means I was at the London School of Economics, and I got involved in certain political activities, and suddenly there was trouble over my grant, and I found I was no longer at the London School of Economics. So I continue my studies here.'

He spoke without bitterness. There was no doubting his commitment, but the violent resentment which had been evident on the night of the filming had gone.

'You want coffee?'

'Love some.'

While John Odange went to fill the kettle, Charles wondered how to proceed. Faced with the young man's quiet sincerity, his pose as a member of the Red Theatre Co-operative diminished to an insulting charade. But he had to get the information somehow.

John Odange returned, plugged the kettle in, sat down in his typing chair and looked straight at Charles. 'So, you were an actor in the West End Television filming and you want to talk to me about it.'

'Yes.' Charles hesitated.

'Hmm. So why would you want to come and talk to me? To tell me I'm a naughty boy to disrupt your precious show? To tell me I should allow other people the right to work? Well, if that's your line, I can argue it through with you point by point. Okay, the evening degenerated. All that fighting with the food was pretty childish. And the fact that someone got killed, no one wanted that. But the basic point we were making, that remains valid. The filming was set up to make fun of the way we live.'

'I don't know exactly that that was the —'

'Now, come on, man. All those Sixties hippies around in the kaftans, they were meant to be funny, right?'

'Well, I suppose so.'

'Right. And the places they live got to be funny too. Okay, let's find somewhere really run down, somewhere really *bad*, that'll get a good laugh.'

'That wasn't the intention in —'

'Listen, man, I found a script lying about in the road. I read it, man.'

In that case, there was not much point in Charles continuing his enfeebled defence. It was probably the first time one of Rod Tisdale's masterpieces had been subjected to serious political scrutiny, and he didn't think it would have come through the test well.

'It said in the Stage Directions, "Film of grotty, condemned street. Establish till audience laughs, then zoom in to shot of Colonel." Now, okay, that's very funny if you don't happen to live here. If you do, it gets kind of insulting.'

'I can see that. I didn't actually come here to —'

'No, no, that's clear. So why did you come here? Now let me see . . . have you come here as a politically-committed actor to say how much you support my actions over stopping the filming and how we're all brothers working for the same glorious revolutionary cause . . . ?'

Here, if ever, was the cue. 'Well, I —'

But John Odange answered his own question. 'No, you don't look the sort for that. Under the sloppiness. man, you're really bourgeois.'

It wasn't said offensively, but with a note of pity. And Charles had an uncomfortable feeling that it was probably an accurate assessment of him. He didn't feel encouraged to proceed with his cover story and start extolling the virtues of solidarity and the coming revolution.

'So what is it? mused John Odange. But he still preferred to supply his own answers to his questions. 'Perhaps your watch disappeared on the night of the filming and you think I stole it . . . ?'

'Good Lord, no. Nothing like that.'

'Don't sound so surprised, man. That's what a lot of people would think. And if you went to the local police station, they'd believe you. In fact, they'd welcome you with open arms. They're just longing to pin something on me, man, and a nice stolen watch could fit the bill nicely.'

'You've had a lot of trouble with them?'

'Always hassles. They think I spend all my time here building bombs, you know. Yes, I've had more than a bellyfull of the pigs recently.'

'Since that Floor Manager died, you mean?'

'Yes. That was a gift for them. If they could pin that on me — wow! they'd all go home happy. They dragged me in and talked to me for a *long* time about that. They were very sorry to have to let me go. Unfortunately, every witness they could rustle up said the same thing — I didn't go near that light at any time during the evening. I didn't arrive till late and then I made such an *exhibition* of myself, my every movement was watched. Were they disappointed? Be a long time before they get another chance like that.'

'Actually, it was about —'

'Oh, I think I get it now.' The large brown eyes opened wide and a huge grin irradiated the face. 'You the little amateur detective investigating the crime? You think you've got new evidence that can really pin it on me?'

'No. Well, yes and no.'

'Which answer to which question? Kind of important to me, you know.'

'It's okay. Yes, I am investigating the murder. No, I have no suspicions of you.'

'Nice to hear that, man. And interesting to hear you call it a murder.'

'I meant "death".'

'Not what you said, man. Classic example of Freudian slip.'

'Maybe.' Charles grinned. The atmosphere between them had relaxed and he felt he could ask his question. He also felt a bit sheepish about the elaborate charade he had prepared for this interview. Direct questions so often succeed in getting direct answers.

But John Odange was still conducting the conversation. 'Okay, I'll tell you anything I can, man. Though I don't think there's much. I didn't see anything odd. I was too busy pouring cream over the fat cats from television.'

'It's not something you saw, it's something you said.'

John Odange shrugged and smiled disarmingly. 'I said a lot that night. Man, did I say a lot that night.'

'Yes, what interests me is that at one point you complained about all the film vehicles and cars that were blocking the roads.'

'Perfectly justified complaint, man. It was like there was a Cup Final on.'

'Yes, I agree. But what I want you to remember is exactly what you said. You gave a great list of all the cars

132

there were blocking streets.'

'All company cars too, I bet.'

'Probably. What I want to know is, was that just a random list you made up, or had you actually seen all the cars you mentioned?'

'What you mean exactly?'

'You said, as I recall, that the streets were full of BMWs and Rovers and Mercs . . .'

'Sure.'

'Did you actually see all those?'

'Certainly did.'

'You also mentioned Daimlers . . .'

John Odange smiled wryly. 'Ah, I think I might have been guilty of a little poetic licence there. I didn't see a Daimler; it just fitted in the rhythm of my rehtoric.'

Oh dear. That didn't augur well for the next question, the important question. 'You also mentioned Bentleys . . .'

'Yes.'

'Does that mean you saw a Bentley?'

'Sure did.' Charles breathed a sigh of relief. 'Yes, there was a dirty great brute of a Bentley hidden behind an old garage in a side street. I saw it as I walked along here.'

'What colour was it?'

'Green. Great big green bugger. Vintage, I'd say.'

There was only one person connected with *The Strutters* who possessed such a car. And that was a person who was supposed to be at home in bed on the night of the filming, while his wife went to the location in a minicab.

Charles had got the information he required. He might have felt a little more satisfaction with his detective skills, tnough, if he had actually interviewed his informant, rather than being interviewed by him.

CHAPTER TWELVE

Barton Rivers had the opportunity on every occasion. When Sadie Wainwright died, he had been in W.E.T. House and would have had plenty of time to arrange the broken railing and help her on her way. The Bentley had been the last car down before Bernard's Rolls on the day Scott

Newton met his end. There was no reason why Barton shouldn't have parked for a few moments out of sight by the gates and slipped back after Bernard Walton had passed to topple the flower-urn. A Bentley made a very effective weapon to run over Rod Tisdale, and its presence near the filming location made it quite possible that Barton had slipped out in the confusion to sabotage the light that killed Robin Laughton.

Four deaths, and he could have done them all. In fact, it made much more sense to suspect Barton than his wife. Charles now felt rather sheepish about his suspicions of Aurelia. Even if her supposed motivation, the protection of her little dog, were not now irrelevant, there was still a strong incongruity of her in the role of murderer. She seemed a remarkably sane woman and, particularly in the case of Rod Tisdale, very unlikely to have been able to commit the crimes, even if she had wished to. So far as Charles knew, she couldn't drive, and the idea of that wispy beauty deliberately running someone over was ridiculous.

And yet it had been definitely to her that Sadie had addressed the words which had stimulated thoughts of murder in the first place. That still fitted rather uncomfortably into the new scenario. Charles's only possible solution was that Aurelia had threatened the PA in a fit of anger, never meaning to carry out her threat, but that Barton, in his unhinged gallantry, had leapt to his wife's defence and done the deed.

And had he had the same motivation for the other crimes? Were they all born of some perverted sense of honour? Or was there perhaps no continuing logic to them at all? Were they just random blows from a madman?

Because there was no doubt that Barton Rivers was mad, but whether there was any method in his madness Charles could not yet work out. The only consistent thread in the deaths was that they were all directed against people connected with *The Strutters* (though, as yet, no member of the cast had been injured). Maybe that fact supplied logic; maybe this massacre was the actor's revenge on all the production staff he had ever worked with. It seemed farfetched.

But if a madman were stage-managing all the deaths,

that did at least explain their random nature. Rod Tisdale's was the only one aimed at a specific target. All the others could have struck at a variety of people, or could have misfired and injured nobody.

But was Barton just gleefully playing the role of an unselective god of destruction, or was there somewhere in his fuddled mind a pattern to the killings?

Another question that worried Charles was the unavoidable one of how much Aurelia knew of her husband's activities. Obviously she wasn't an accomplice, but, as the deaths mounted, she must have come to suspect something. If Barton had stopped and slipped back to move the urn at Bernard's place, even if she didn't think it odd at the time, subsequent events must have made her suspicious. Equally, she must have known that he was out in the car at the time of Rod Tisdale's death.

And yet she seemed to want the business sorted out and ended. Charles could not forget her appeal to him which had filled him with such crusading fervour. 'And I do appreciate what you're doing for us. If there is a solution to all this, then I'm sure you're the one to find it.'

In the light of his recent thinking, her words took on a different emphasis. The important word became 'us'. I appreciate what you're doing for *us*. Was she tacitly admitting that the problem was one that she and her husband shared? That she knew what he was doing, but was powerless to stop him?

Another thought followed hard on that. He remembered when he had asked whether Cocky had been poisoned, Aurelia's face had registered shock. Perhaps the dog had been killed, and perhaps Barton had done it, as a threat to buy his wife's continuing silence. Maybe he had threatened her own life too. Charles knew that many things happened inside marriages which were invisible to outsiders. Was it fear that kept Aurelia Howarth so tightly bound to her lunatic husband?

He didn't think he was going to find out any answers to these questions until *The Strutters* got back into production again. Three of the deaths had taken place on production days, and the fourth, Rod Tisdale's, had been right in the middle of a very busy rehearsal schedule. Charles somehow didn't think much would happen until they started work on the next batch of shows. And then he was determined to watch Barton Rivers like a hawk whenever he came near the production. There was still no real evidence to trap the madman. But Charles was determined to find some before there was another 'accident'.

He got a batch of new scripts through the post a couple of days before the next readthrough. Willy and Sam Tennison had made predictable changes in the show's direction. Not only, as anticipated, had they brought in a semi-permanent girlfriend for the Nick Coxhill figure, they had even got the Colonel and Mrs Strutter exchanging darlings like newly-weds. This softening of their relationship weakened the aggressive crustiness of the Colonel's character and, since that was the main basis of the series' comedy, Charles thought George Birkitt might have something to say about it at the next readthrough.

But Peter Lipscombe must have been happy with the scripts or he wouldn't have issued them. Though it seemed to Charles that the producer was so much under the writers' spell that he would never dare find any fault with their scripts.

Episode Eight was, for those trained to spot such things, a version of a plot that Willy and Sam Tennison had used in an episode of *Oh, What a Pair of Au Pairs!* In that, a Japanese family had moved in next door to the au pair-owning young couple and, after a lot of misunderstandings, jokes about tiny transistorised instruments and the line 'There's a nip in the air', a kind of peaceful coexistence had been achieved, symbolised by the Japanese family's gift of a geisha girl as a third au pair (an hilarious consequence if ever there was one).

The Strutters version of this saga of racial stereotypes had a Japanese family moving next door to Colonel and Mrs Strutter. The same misunderstandings, jokes about tiny transistorised instruments and the line 'There's a nip in the air' ensued, but a less total rapprochement resulted. In a pay-off which was, by Willy and Sam Tennison's standards, satirical, the Japanese family presented Colonel Strutter with a samurai sword and, when he asked what it was for, told him that it was for committing hara-kiri

136

when he got too depressed about Japanese car imports.

Charles predicted that George Birkitt wouldn't like that either. But he paid scant attention to the scripts, because by the same post arrived a much more interesting communication. It came from his agent, Maurice Skellern, which already made it a rarity, and it contained a very large cheque, which made it rarer still. It was in fact the money owing to him for the first batch of *Strutters*, which Maurice, as was his wont, had sat on for some weeks. But also, as was his wont, he had not forgotten to deduct his commission.

Even so, it really was rather a gratifying amount of money. So long as he didn't consider paying tax bills or anything like that (which he didn't), he felt quite well off.

The day before the next readthrough, he started to worry about what Barton Rivers was going to do next, and to doubt his capacity to avert it. He couldn't really watch the man all the time; it would be simpler if he had someone to help him.

He rang Gerald Venables. Polly, the solicitor's secretary, whose sexy voice always gave Charles erotic fantasies, put him through.

'Hello, Charles, how are things going?'

'Not so bad. I think I may have a line on the deaths.'

'Good, good,' said Gerald breezily. But he didn't sound very interested. Not his usual panting schoolboy reaction to talk of murder.

'Perhaps we could meet and talk about it.'

'Love to. Trouble is, I'm a bit tied up at the moment. In a couple of days I'm —'

'Thing is, I think you could help me.' This appeal shouldn't fail. Gerald was usually delighted to get involved in a murder investigation. Real crime had so much more to offer than sorting out show-biz contracts.

'Love to, love to. Trouble is, we're off on holiday day after tomorrow.'

'Ah.'

'School holidays just started, you see.'

'Going far?'

'Have to go some way these days to get away from the crowds.

'Where?' asked Charles with jealous resignation.

'Seychelles.'

'Just the Seychelles?'

'Mmm. Well, if you only get one holiday a year, you like to be able to guarantee the weather.'

'But you don't only get one holiday a year.'

'No, that's true.'

'You're always off on bloody holiday.'

'Have to have the odd break, you know. Recharge the batteries. I do work for it,' Gerald added in an aggrieved voice.

'Hmm.'

'You ought to have a holiday. Go off with Frances somewhere. Are you speaking to her at the moment?'

'Haven't for some time.'

'Oh dear.'

'No great rift. Just haven't got round to it.'

'Well, you should.'

'I will.'

'Anyway, about these deaths . . . are you going to bring me up to date?'

'No. It'll keep. I'll tell you when you get back. Probably be a few more by then.'

'Good. I'm only away the fortnight.'

'Just the fortnight?'

'Yes.'

'Right. I must say, as a Dr Watson, you're hopeless. Sherlock Holmes never had this trouble. He didn't have his faithful acolyte zooming off to the Seychelles whenever his assistance was needed.'

'No, but on the other hand, he solved crimes.'

Charles thought about what Gerald had said when he put the phone down. Not the final gibe, that hadn't hurt, such rudeness was well established between them; no, he thought about what Gerald had said about Frances.

It would be rather good to go on holiday with her. He was already getting bored with Jay Lewis. The sex was all right, but there was a limit to how much quotation from the luminaries of West End Television he could take.

Frances, though . . . They'd always said, in the old days, that when they could afford it, they'd go to Greece. Just the two of them, without Juliet. Thanks to the cheque from Maurice, he now reckoned he could afford it. And Juliet, in her late twenties with a husband and twin sons, no longer presented a problem.

He rang Frances's number. There was no reply. He'd try again.

He was just going back to his bedsitter when the pay-phone rang. The Swedes all being out, he returned to answer it. Some cock-eyed logic suggested it might be Frances ringing him back.

It wasn't. It was a man's voice he didn't recognise.

'Hello, could I speak to Charles Paris?'

'Speaking.'

'Oh, hello, my name's Gregory Watts . . .'

'Oh yes . . .' It didn't ring any bells for Charles.

'I'm a bookdealer specialising in detective fiction.'

'Oh yes.' With more understanding.

'Just talking to a friend of mine who runs a bookshop in Charing Cross Road, and he said you'd been looking for an R.Q. Wilberforce . . .'

'Yes, I was. In a vague sort of way.'

'Well, look, I've got this first edition of *Death Takes A Short Cut*. Very Good Condition. 1938 it is, but of course you'd know that.'

'Um, oh, er, yes.'

'If you do want it, I'm asking five pounds.'

'Ah.'

'I've got other collectors who might be interested. But I rang you first, because my friend said you only collected R.Q. Wilberforce.'

'Well . . .' It rather appealed, the idea of being the nation's specialist in Wilberforciania. Even if it wasn't true.

'Have you met the old boy, by the way?'

'Which old boy?'

'R.Q. Wilberforce. He's still about. Must be in his eighties. I wrote to him to see if he'd got any old editions he wanted to get rid of.'

'Ah.'

'He said he'd got rid of them all. I didn't believe him. Not many of these authors want to part with their private copies of their own works. Mind you, the widows often don't care so much, if you come in with a reasonable offer.'

'Really? No, no, I haven't met him. Don't know much about him.' Anything about him, in fact.

'Well, do you want to buy it?'

Charles couldn't remember exactly why he had thought the book important. It was part of some train of thought that had been shunted off into a siding to make way for the Intercity express conviction of Barton Rivers' guilt. On the other hand, he did feel fairly flush and this bloke had taken the trouble to ring up . . .

'Yes, please, I would like it.'

'Okay, well, if you can send me a cheque for £5.32 — that's with postage — I'll send the book as soon as I receive the money.'

'Fine.'

Be nice to have something to read while he watched to see who Barton Rivers tried to eliminate next.

He felt a chill. Of course it was possible that the old madman might start on members of *The Strutters* cast.

CHAPTER THIRTEEN

'Now please don't worry. Everything's going to be okay,' Peter Lipscombe assured the cast at the readthrough on the 27th July, 'but I should just put you in the picture about the news on the industrial front. You'll have heard that there was a one-day strike last Monday, and there have also been one or two other go-slows and things happening, but I think the atmosphere's clearing now, and I don't think we need worry about our recording next Friday. You may find odd things happening in the W.E.T. building — I mean, for instance there may not be any canteen service and the bar may suddenly be closed . . .'

A communal groan broke from the cast.

'. . . But I think basically everything's going to be okay. We'll get the show made, don't you worry about that. Now one thing I should tell you — I don't think it's likely to happen, but we should be prepared for any eventuality — when we get into the studio, we may have to rehearse/ record the show during the day. You see, at the moment — and I'm sure this will have changed by next Friday — at the moment the security men have got an overtime ban on, which means that they won't work evenings, which means we can't have an audience in the studio because of safety regulations. So if that ban hasn't been lifted — and I'm sure it will have been — we'll get the schedule changed and do the show during the day . . .'

'And dub the laughs on afterwards?' asked Bob Tomlinson.

'Yes,' replied the producer with distaste.

'Good,' said Bob Tomlinson.

'Okay, sure it won't happen, but thought you'd like to know. Oh, one other thing about the studio. We're not in Studio A this week, we're in B.'

'The small one?' asked George Birkitt, affronted.

'Small*er*,' conceded the producer.

'Why?'

'Well, Wragg and Bowen are in the big studio.'

'Why?'

'It is a big prestige show.'

'And what about us? Aren't we a big prestige show?'

'Of course, of course. But not quite *as* big a prestige show as Wragg and Bowen.'

'Just because of the bloody money they're being paid . . . George Birkitt muttered darkly.

'You finished?' asked Bob Tomlinson, with his customary lack of grace.

'More or less,' said Peter Lipscombe.

'Right, let's get this rubbish read. You ready on the watch, girl?'

Jay Lewis was ready for the readthrough, but George Birkitt wasn't. 'I'm sorry, before we start, there are a few things in this script we've got to change.'

'Why?' asked Bob Tomlinson belligerently.

'Because they're just wrong. I mean I've spent seven episodes of this series — not to mention all the *What'll the Neighbours* . . . before it — building up Colonel Strutter into a recognisable, rounded comic character, and now I'm handed a script in which not only does he have considerably less lines than in previous episodes, but the ones he does have are unfunny and out of character.'

'Oh, but we've worked so hard to maintain the character,' wailed Sam Tennison, dressed today in a Mister Men

T-shirt and strawberry coloured jeans. 'Haven't we, darling?'

'Yes, indeed, darling,' concurred Willy Tennison, also dressed today in a Mister Men T-shirt and strawberry coloured jeans.

'Then obviously you just haven't worked hard enough,' said George Birkitt. 'I mean, I know Colonel Strutter, and these lines aren't Colonel Strutter. I can't learn lines that are out of character.'

'You can't learn lines that are *in* character,' was the thought that went through every mind in the room. But nobody said it.

'I mean, for a start, since when has Colonel Strutter called Mrs Strutter "darling"?'

'Oh, but all married couples call each other "darling". Don't they, darling?'

'They certainly do, darling.'

'Not Colonel Strutter. He wouldn't go in for that sort of sentimental nonsense. He never calls his wife anything.'

'But he has to call her *something*,' complained Sam Tennison.

'Well, he doesn't.'

'But everyone calls everyone *something*. Don't they, darling?'

'They most certainly do, darling.'

'Anyway, that's only a detail,' George Birkitt steamrollered on. 'The plot is full of silly things too, which are just out of keeping with the rest of the series that we've already made. I mean, that business at the end with the samurai sword. Have you ever *met* a Japanese with a samurai sword?' He turned to the Japanese actor who was playing the Strutters' new neighbour. 'I mean, have you got any samurai swords?'

'Yes, many,' replied the Japanese with a polite smile.

'Well, that's neither here not there. As a pay-off for an episode of *The Strutters* it's just hopelessly out of keeping.'

'Oh no,' murmured Mort Verdon, who was sitting by Charles. 'Don't cut the samurai sword. I spent most of last week finding somewhere that would hire the thing to us. They're about as easy to come by as a banana in a convent.'

'Now come on,' Peter Lipscombe was saying bonhomously. 'I'm sure everything's really okay with this script. Just change the odd word here and there and . . .'

Charles relaxed. Barton Rivers had delivered Aurelia to the rehearsal and then driven away. If anything was going to happen, it wouldn't be yet a while.

Idly he wondered what form the next attack would take. Shooting . . . ? Stabbing . . . ? Bombing . . . ?

He also wondered idly who would be its target.

But the week passed very quietly at the Paddington Jewish Boys' Club. Those whose work took them into W.E.T. House, like Mort Verdon, came back speaking of strikes and rumours of strikes, but the atmosphere in the rehearsal room remained peaceful. All of the *Strutters* team had benefited from the few days' rest and seemed relaxed. George Birkitt, whose objections to the script had really only been a way of asserting himself, was content with a few minor word-changes. The offending 'darlings' were excised, which made the script a revolutionary new departure in the literary careers of Willy and Sam Tennison, and George became quite mellow. He didn't really mind about having less lines than usual; if the truth were told, he was quite relieved — there was now a chance he might be able to learn them. But the tantrum had been necessary to him. As he said to Charles, 'Well, you know I'm the last person on earth to throw a scene, but occasionally one does have to put one's foot down and remind them who one is, or they trample all over you . . . er, one.'

He had also been persuaded that the pay-off should be left unaltered. This was not because he thought it was right, but to avoid trouble; he had finally accepted it with a don't-say-I-didn't-warn-you shrug. After all, if the whole show was likely to be dubbed, it didn't really matter whether the jokes were funny or not. The viewing audience would laugh with recorded hilarity just as much as they would with the sounds of a so-called live audience.

Because, as the week progressed, there seemed less and less chance of the show's being recorded on the normal schedule. The security men's go-slow was unlikely to be resolved; the worry was how many more unions were likely to join them. The threat of the strike that Charles had jokingly predicted, of ITV staff for greater disparity of pay from BBC staff, loomed larger.

As a result of this, the rehearsal room saw more of Peter Lipscombe than it had since Bob Tomlinson took over as director. The producer appeared almost every day, bringing news of fresh possibilities and contingency plans. Nothing dented his Little Noddy image, though. Everything was still going to be okay, they were still working on the most exciting series to have hit television since Logie Baird's early experiments. Maybe the pitch of these assertions rose to a more hysterical level as the week went on, but nothing stopped them pouring out.

And everything seemed to be normal with Dame Aurelia Howarth and her husband. The senile homicide delivered his wife to the rehearsal room in the Bentley and picked her up at the end of the day's work. On no occasion did he come inside the building.

The only significant moment came when Aurelia, who always did the correct thing, asked Bob Tomlinson, 'Darling, if this beastly go-slow happens and we have to rehearse/record the show through the day, do you mind if Barton sits in and watches? He does so enjoy coming to the recordings.'

'No, that's all right, love,' said the director, who, in spite of his resistance to show-biz schmaltz, had, over the weeks, like everyone else, developed a soft spot for Dob Howarth.

She turned to Charles, who was standing nearby, and gave him the exclusive benefit of her smile. 'How are things?' she asked lightly.

'Getting somewhere,' he said confidently, the intimacy between knight errant and damsel in distress re-established.

Aurelia looked up with sudden understanding. Once again he felt sure that she suspected Barton too.

And he also felt sure that, if the old lunatic was going to strike again, he would do so on the studio day.

Just as he was about to leave Hereford Road for rehearsal the day before the recording, Charles received a package through the letter-box. It was in a padded brown envelope and for a moment he couldn't imagine what it might be. Then the Kew postmark and the feel of the contents told him it must be his rare copy of R.Q. Wilberforce's *Death Takes A Short Cut*.

Because he was late, he shoved the package into his

pocket and caught a cab to the Paddington Jewish Boys'
Club. The cab was just another example of how having
money in his pocket made him feel wealthy. He still hadn't
managed to get through to Frances about the Greek idea;
must try again.

Not much rehearsal ever gets done the day before studio,
because the timing revolves around the Crew Run. This is
the occasion when, as actors often put it, 'the anoraks
move in'. In other words, all the studio staff, cameramen,
sound-boom operators and so on, come to see the show in
rehearsed form and follow it in their camera scripts (often
typed up by the PA into the small hours of the previous
night).

The Crew Run on this occasion was scheduled for twelve
noon and, as the hour drew near, tension mounted. No one
was quite sure of the latest on the industrial front and
there were constant calls for various union members to go
to meetings, which might or might not lead to strike action.
Until all the crew turned up, it would not be known
whether the show could go ahead. In their present militant
mood, the technicians were liable to regard one member's
absence as an instance of undermanning which would not
allow the rest of them to proceed.

Mort Verdon twittered around with gloomy cautionary
anecdotes from W.E.T. House. How the waitresses in the
Executive Dining Room had walked out, leaving the
Catering Manager to serve a lunch party of ten, given by
Nigel Frisch. How a fellow Stage Manager had been having
his bacon roll handed over the canteen counter when the
call for a meeting came over the loudspeakers, and how the
sweet-smelling breakfast had been whisked back from
under his hungry nose. How a particularly bolshie studio
team had insisted on reboiling a kettle and remaking tea
for every rehearsal of a brief scene in a drama production.
Mort got very dramatic about it all.

But gradually the anoraks assembled. Peter Lipscombe
was for once silent and even anxious as he counted the
crew members. One by one they came in through the
rehearsal room door and, with the instinct of their breed,
homed in on the coffee machine and tins of biscuits.

So the Crew Run was achieved. It even went quite well.
George Birkitt remembered most of his lines. Peter

Lipscombe thought it was a terrific episode and the whole series was jolly exciting.

Afterwards, as everyone disbanded, the mood was cheerful. The crew had been friendly and no one doubted that the show would get made the next day.

George Birkitt, flushed with the success of his feat of memory, asked if he could buy Charles a drink. Charles conceded the requisite permission. He felt relaxed. Nothing would happen till the studio day.

'Stupid thing came up the other day,' said George Birkitt with a sheepish grin, as they sat outside a mews pub drinking pints of Guinness. 'Had a call from the headmaster of my old school — asked if I'd open the school fête. I must have "arrived", they usually get some retired Colonel or something.'

'It's the Colonel Strutter image.'

'I suppose it is. Flattering in a way, mind.'

'Are you going to do it?'

'Oh, I'm not sure. Depends what else I have on round the date. I've referred him to my agent.'

'Oh.'

'Well, you do have to be bloody careful. I mean, you do one of these things as a favour, word gets out, and suddenly they're all clamouring round.'

'I hadn't thought of that.'

'Believe me, it happens. Anyway, it's easier if my agent sorts out the financial side.'

'I hadn't thought of that either.'

'Got to be canny, Charles, got to be canny.'

They both drank deeply into their Guinness. George Birkitt continued, 'Rang my wife the other day.'

'Oh, really?'

'Do you know her? Stephanie Roscoe.'

'I know her as an actress. I didn't know you were married.'

'Oh yes. We've been separated for a few years. You know, her career really took off when she got that part in the Royals telly series.'

'I read about it.'

'Made life very difficult for us. I was going through a bad patch, you know, professionally. Puts strain on a marriage, when one partner's very successful and in demand, and the other . . . ain't. So, after a lot of fighting, we split up. Best thing at the time.'

'Hmm.'

'You're divorced, aren't you?'

'Not actually divorced. Just separated.'

'Uh-huh.'

'I found an actor's life incompatible with matrimony.'

'It's difficult, certainly.'

'Must be even more difficult if you're both in the business. When you've got professional rivalry to add to the other pressures.'

'Doesn't help, Charles. You very rarely get show-biz marriages where the two careers balance exactly. For every pair of Lunts, there must be a hundred Dobs and Bartons.'

'Yes.'

'Of course, I was never jealous of Stephanie. Problems were just logistical. I mean, she was — is — a sweet girl, but really no great shakes as an actress. Just had a couple of lucky breaks. So jealousy was never really appropriate.'

'No. Haven't heard much about her recently. What's she been up to?'

'Not a lot, poor darling. Got a bit over-exposed, I think, with the Royals thing. So I thought I'd just ring, see how she was.'

'And how was she?'

'Fine, fine. Pity about this damned go-slow. I was going to ask her to come along to one of these recordings.'

So that she can see George Birkitt's name above the title, thought Charles, as the other continued, 'Still, I'm taking her out to dinner in a couple of days. See if there's anything left.'

'Hope there is, for your sake.'

George Birkitt shrugged. 'Doesn't worry me one way or the other. Just be interesting to see her, though.'

'Yes.'

'Strange, you know, during the time she was successful with that series, while I was spending a lot of time sitting around at home while she was off at rehearsals and premieres and things, I got really paranoid about it. You know, began to doubt my own abilities.' He laughed. 'Even started to believe Stephanie's publicity and think she was more talented than I was. Huh, but strange how quickly one gets like that. Most difficult part in the world, second fiddle, specially for a man.'

'But you don't have any worries about that now?'

'Good Lord, no. Everything's turned out fine recently. I really think this series could do me a lot of good, you know.'

'I'm sure it will. Same again?'

'That would be very pleasant.'

As Charles went into the pub with the empty glasses, he mulled over what George had said about the pressures of being second fiddle. A lifetime of it could unhinge someone. Suppose you married a wife when you were both at about the same level in the business. And then you watched her rise to international success, while your career made no noticeable advance. You saw her become the toast of London and New York, you heard her name on everyone's lips, you saw her picture everywhere. You stood by while she became a pin-up of the Forces, you witnessed her career mature with her years, you saw her break into television with the same unerring success, you read the announcement that she had been made a Dame of the British Empire . . .

That kind of pressure could drive a man insane. And who knew what revenge he might take on the world which had put him in a position of such constant inequality.

He wondered again where Barton Rivers would strike next.

With four pints of Guinness inside him, he wandered back to Hereford Road through the bleary sunlight. It was really too nice an afternoon to go back to the bedsitter, but he had a vague intention of ringing Frances. The school of which she was headmistress must have broken up by now. It would be good to speak to her. George's words about the pressures of show business marriages had reminded him of the advantages of his own.

Then, after he had spoken to her, he might go out to the park. Walk round the Serpentine, maybe.

It was when he was inside the stuffy bedsitter that he became aware of the bulky package in his pocket. Oh yes, of course, his R.Q. Wilberforce. In his Guinness-sodden state, he couldn't really think why he had it.

He pieced it together slowly. Oh yes, it had started with that book Romney Kirkstall had had, the biography of Aurelia Howarth in which there had been a still from an aborted film called *Death Takes A Short Cut*. Then later Romney said he'd seen a copy of a book with that title in a Charing Cross Road bookshop Barton Rivers had recommended to him. So Charles had gone to the bookshop, been put in touch with Gregory Watts and . . . yes, yes, of course.

He took the brown padded package out. There was a little red plastic tag which would open the bag along a line of perforations.

He took hold of the tag and pulled it.

CHAPTER FOURTEEN

DEATH TAKES A SHORT CUT
by
R.Q. WILBERFORCE

CHAPTER I
THE TRAVELLER'S RETURN

Maltravers Ratcliffe had risen and broken his fast early, so that he was already installed behind his desk, with a long black cigarette holder between his teeth, reading through his accumulated correspondence, when his wife appeared at the library door.

'So my bonny has come back to me,' she announced with joy.

'Over the sea to Skye,' he rejoined merrily, as he rose to greet her. 'Except, in my case, it was over the sea and through the sky. I came on the aeroplane to Croydon. Podd brought the Bentley down to meet me at the 'drome, and we fairly flew again as we drove back here!'

'You should have wakened me on your arrival.'

'No, no, Eithne my love. Even the nonpareil of beauty can reap benefit from a little beauty-sleep.'

Nor was his description fanciful; Eithne Ratcliffe was

*possessed of a beauty that would quicken the blood in any
man's veins. Though slight, she was perfectly proportioned,
and her carriage was superb. The golden hair that was her
chiefest glory had been cut in the modern style, but its
waves owed nothing to the artifice of coiffeurs. And her
eyes! What eyes! Their hue of purest blue would have
made a cornflower despondent; sapphires could offer but
feeble comparison to them.*

*'Was your business in Paris successfully concluded?'
she enquired of her handsome spouse.*

*'Successfully enough,' he conceded carelessly. 'Although,
as is ever the case, I trapped the small fry in the certain
knowledge that the big fish swam away unscathed.'*

'Was it . . . ?' Eithne questioned tremulously.

*'Our old enemy?' Maltravers nodded with gravity. 'That
same Teutonic devil was behind this latest outrage. Backed
by an international conglomerate of Jewish bankers, he
was planning to flood the gold bullion market with
counterfeit ingots. Had he succeeded, he'd have crippled all
the major economies of the Western world! Shares would
have gone down to cat's meat prices and hundreds of
perfectly decent small houses would have gone smash!'*

*'But you prevented the swindle?' demanded Eithne, her
wonderful eyes sparkling as she looked at her husband.*

*'Oh yes, I scotched his scheme easily. It was like eating
jam. Once I had worked out that someone must be manipu-
lating prices on the Bourse, I found out who it was first
pop. A little Jewish thimblerigger, who I may say won't be
seeing much scenery except the inside of a prison for the
next twenty years. The Sûreté were very grateful. I've
been awarded one of their "croix d'honneurs".'*

Charles' concentration on the words wavered, but his
interest was fiercely aroused. He skimmed some verbose
description of Maltravers Ratcliffe's cricketing prowess and
a long, somewhat precious discussion about where the
couple should spend the weekend. This was resolved at
the end of the first chapter . . .

*With a merry laugh, Maltravers cried, 'I've had my fill of
crime for a while! Let's away to Derbyshire to play cricket.
I happen to know Lord Wainscott fields a scratch team*

150

that's none so dusty. Tell Podd and Smithers to commence packing for us immediately! We'll take the Bentley and they can follow along in the Sunbeam. Oh, and tell Wallace to prepare a luncheon-basket, so that we are free to lunch where the scenery's good. Then we'll leap into the Bentley, my angel, point the bonnet towards Derbyshire, and be there in two twos!'

The second chapter assembled a house party of suspects at Wainscott Hall, in the time-honoured style of its genre. One of them, a foreign gentleman called Mr Akbar, did not endear himself to the rest of the guests . . .

The presence of this last personage was an unaccountable mystery. Neither his appearance nor his manners qualified him as a likely social acquaintance of Lord Wainscott, and yet the peer seemed ready, nay, eager, to welcome the foreigner into that proverbial castle of the Englishman, his home. Mr Akbar did not commend himself to the Ratcliffes by appearing at dinner in a silken commerbund of the hue favoured by Romish cardinals and diamond studs of such ostentatious size that they might have looked less out of place amongst the regalia of a Babylonian Coronation! And Maltravers Ratcliffe, in front of whom the newcomer pushed as they proceeded to dinner, was not a little shocked to feel his nostrils assailed by a distinct whiff of perfume!

All that the book needed now, apart from a plan of the ground floor of Wainscott Hall (which soon appeared duly printed in the text), was a crime. After dinner Maltravers and Eithne Ratcliffe repaired to the billiard room . . .

'You know, my love, there's something deuced rummy going on here,' mused Maltravers as he chalked his cue. 'Deuced rummy. Something that makes my flesh creep. Do you feel it too?'
    His wife answered in the affirmative.
    'It's something to do with that gigolo, Akbar. I've a feeling he's out to spoke somebody's wheel. And what's more . . . I've a feeling I've seen the bounder somewhere before.'

At that moment Maltravers Ratcliffe froze, his face suffused by a ghastly pallor, his eyes transfixed by some object on the floor.

'Oh no,' he breathed. 'Oh no, oh no, oh no!'

He moved forward and picked up a monocle, whose silver setting was curiously wrought in the shape of a coiled snake. 'See, he has left his visiting card.'

'Are you sure?' murmured Eithne, unwilling to accept the sheer ugliness of the truth.

'Sure,' her husband confirmed with unearthly calmness. 'Yes, it's von Strutter!'

Eithne Ratcliffe gasped. Their arch-enemy! Here, at Wainscott Hall!

'What's behind there?' Maltravers demanded, pointing to a door in front of which the monocle had lain.

'That's where Lord Wainscott keeps his collection.'

'Quick!'

He tried the door. It was locked, and there was no sign of a key. Fortunately he always carried a set of pick-locks, fashioned for him by the versatile Podd, and to open the door was a matter of moments.

One look inside sufficed to tell him all!

'Don't look, my love, don't look!' he commanded Eithne as he entered the room.

The walls were hung with many splendours of the Orient, but he had eyes for none of these. All he saw was the ghastly spectacle staining the fine Turkey carpet in the middle of the room.

It was the offensive Mr Akbar, destined never more to give offence!

He lay face down on the floor. Upright from the back of his coat rose the bloody blade of a Japanese samurai sword!

CHAPTER FIFTEEN

The effects of four pints of Guinness vanished. Charles's mind was working very clearly. And fast.

It was incongruous, and yet it might be true. Could the pattern to this apparently meaningless sequence of deaths lie in a series of forgotten detective stories?

There were too many coincidences for him to dismiss the idea with his customary cynicism. The old still from the never-completed film of *Death Takes A Short Cut* told him that Barton Rivers and Aurelia Howarth had once been cast as Maltravers and Eithne Ratcliffe, and the old man's bizarre dress and style of speech suggested that in some mad way he was still playing the part. It made sense of the white flannels and all the inconsequential cricketing jargon, as well as Barton's permanent air of demented gallantry.

But the greatest coincidence was in the name, von Strutter. There had to be some connection there. If somewhere in the fogs of Barton Rivers' mind, he was convinced he had an arch-enemy called von Strutter, he might well seek revenge on a television series which was called *The Strutters*. It was lunatic logic, but it was the only form of logic Charles had so far been able to impose on the random accidents.

The most chilling thing he had read, though, was R.Q. Wilberforce's choice of murder weapon. The coincidence of a samurai sword in the book and in the script of the next day's *Strutters* episode seemed to offer too much temptation to Barton Rivers' insane motivation. The accident with the sword must be averted.

But Charles needed more information. All he had so far was an idea, a new theory into which some of the known facts fitted. Many more would have to fall into place before he could dignify the theory with the title of a solution.

That meant finding out a lot more about the books of R.Q. Wilberforce. He went to the payphone on the landing.

'Hello, Gregory Watts.'

'This is Charles Paris.'

'Oh, good afternoon. Did you get the book all right?'

'Yes, thank you.'

'What else can I do for you?'

'I seem to remember when we spoke, you said R.Q. Wilberforce was still alive.'

'Was last year, certainly.'

'Look, I need to contact him very urgently. Have you got a phone number for him?'

'No, I've got an address. Incidentally, when I wrote to him, I wrote to R.Q. Wilberforce, but his reply was very

153

firmly signed in his real name, so perhaps you should use that.'

'You mean R.Q. Wilberforce is a pseudonym?'

'Certainly.' Watts laughed. 'I can't imagine too many people are actually called R.Q. Wilberforce.'

'It's possible.'

'Oh yes. Mind you, his real name is pretty odd, too.'

'Oh. What is it?'

'Barton Rivers.' There was a long silence. 'Are you still there, Mr Paris?'

'Yes, I . . . yes. Good God.'

'Shall I give you his address?'

'Yes . . . no. I mean, no, I don't need it now.'

'Oh, but I thought . . .'

'No, what I do need are copies of his books. All of them. And fast.'

'I told you, that's the only one I've got — or rather had. They're pretty rare.'

'But they must exist somewhere. Don't you know of any libraries or . . .'

'I suppose they might be around in a library, but you could spend weeks looking.'

'I've got to find them. It's really important.'

'Hmm . . . Well, the only thing I can suggest — I don't know if any of them would have any — but there are one or two collectors who specialise in detective fiction. You could ask.'

'Anything's worth trying.'

Gregory Watts gave him three names and phone numbers.

Stanley Harvey's cottage in Hampstead was, like his speech, precise to the point of being precious. On the telephone he had admitted with pride to being the possessor of an almost complete set of R.Q. Wilberforce, but he had been unwilling to have them inspected that evening. Charles had to use all his powers of persuasion and even resort to the phrase (for once used in a literal sense) 'a matter of life and death', before he achieved grudging consent. 'But I'm going out at eight,' said Stanley Harvey, 'so you'll have to be through by then.'

And no, there was no possibility of Charles borrowing any of the books.

154

When he opened the front door, Stanley Harvey lived up to the impression of his voice and cottage. He was a dapper little man in his early sixties, with a white goatee beard. A tweed Norfolk jacket and a Meerschaum pipe gave a Sherlockian image, which was reinforced by prints on the walls, models and memorabilia of the great detective.

Stanley Harvey seemed unimpressed by Charles Paris. 'This is really extremely inconvenient. I hope you meant what you said about it being important.'

'You must believe me. It is. It's far too complicated to explain but it is important.'

Stanley Harvey sniffed. 'I rang Gregory Watts and he confirmed that he had given you my number. Can't be too careful. The collection is pretty valuable and I can't let *just anyone* in.'

The emphasis, and the look that accompanied it, suggested he suspected Charles might be *just anyone* and still contemplated refusing admission. 'Gregory Watts said you were an R.Q. Wilberforce collector.'

'Hardly. I've only got one of the books. *Death Takes A Short Cut.*'

Stanley Harvey gave a superior smile. 'Oh, I've got that, of course. I've got five of them, and there only ever were the six.'

'First editions?' Charles felt he had to ask, only to give Stanley Harvey the satisfaction of saying a supercilious 'Of course.'

It had been a good question, because now Stanley Harvey's desire to show off his collection was greater than his distrust of his visitor. 'Come through,' he said curtly.

They went to the back of the cottage and through a passage to what appeared to be a modern extension. As they walked, Stanley Harvey continued to parade his knowledge. 'Of course, the reason R.Q. Wilberforces are so rare is that so few were printed.'

'Oh?' said Charles humbly.

'Yes, he never really caught on as an author. He was too larky and the plotting was too slack, I believe. He had the books printed at his own expense.'

'Really?'

'Oh yes.' Stanley Harvey had perked up now he saw what a humble student he had to lecture. Yes, he must have been a schoolteacher, he obviously enjoyed pontificating so much. A schoolteacher who had come into money.

Quite a lot of money, Charles reckoned when they went into the library. It was a purpose-built circular room. Packed bookshelves rose to the ceiling, alternating with tall windows protected with metal grids. All their books, arranged with the pernickety neatness that characterised their owner, were hard-backs of this century.

Charles made suitably appreciative noises.

'Yes, not bad,' said Stanley Harvey smugly. 'One of the largest private collections in the world, so I believe.'

'Of what?' Charles couldn't resist saying.

'Detective fiction. All first editions of course. I have my own private cataloguing system.'

Yes, you would.

'Conan Doyles along there — complete set of English and American firsts. Agatha Christie, the same. Raymond Chandler . . . Dorothy Sayers, of course. Simenons in the original, English editions and some selected translations and —'

'What about R.Q. Wilberforces?' asked Charles. It was twenty past six, the eight o'clock curfew was approaching fast, and he felt a desperate urgency to find out if he was on to something or just caught up in an elaborate fantasy.

'Yes,' said Stanley Harvey, with a *moue* of annoyance. 'Of course. Right, if that's all you're interested in, over here.'

He moved across the room and pointed to a row of matching blue spines. 'Here we are. R.Q. Wilberforce. The only one I haven't been able to track down yet is *Death Takes A Back Seat*. But here we have *Death Takes A Tumble, Death Takes The Wrong Turning, Death Takes A Drive, Death Takes A Stand* and *Death Takes A Short Cut*. I also have some manuscripts and drafts of stuff that was never published, if that's of interest.' He gestured towards a rank of metal filing cabinets.

'Did you collect them all one at a time?'

'No, not the R.Q. Wilberforces, actually. I do with most of the stuff, get it from publishers or through dealers, but in fact I got all this lot together. Just after the war I wrote to R.Q. Wilberforce and asked if he'd got any material he wanted to get rid of. To my surprise he sent me

156

the lot. With a very strange letter. Said that he had been going to throw it all away, said that the War had changed everything, that there was no time for frivolity any more, that life had been shown up in its true colours and it was a tragic business. He said that R.Q. Wilberforce was dead and he never wanted to hear anything about him again. The letter was very odd, sounded a bit unbalanced.'

'Did he sign his own name?'

'He signed R.Q. Wilberforce, I don't know whether that was his name or not. I've got the letter filed if —'

'It doesn't matter.'

Stanley Harvey smiled a self-satisfied smile. 'So I got a nice little haul there for nothing. Shows what a letter arriving at the right time can do. Always worth writing a lot of letters if you're building up a collection.'

'Yes.' Charles looked at his watch. Half-past six. And he looked at the thickness of the five blue books on the shelf. 'Look, perhaps you could save me a bit of time. All I need to find out is about the deaths in the books. Perhaps you can remember something of the plots . . .'

Stanley Harvey looked at him in amazement and stroked his little beard. 'Good Lord, no. I only collect this stuff, I don't read it.'

Stanley Harvey perched watchfully at his desk in the middle of the library while Charles did his reasearch. The circular room strengthened the impression of a spider at the centre of his web, as did the little man's suspicious eyes. He clearly expected Charles to try to leave with an illicit Margery Allingham under his jacket.

But once he got into the books, Charles was too intrigued to be inhibited by any hostile spectator. He read with fascination as the pattern he had suspected unfolded in all its lunacy.

He soon realised that he wouldn't have to read all the text. The relevant bits were not hard to find.

He opened each book and checked the date to confirm their sequence. There was a dedication in each one, too. In the first, *Death Takes A Tumble*, it read 'To Darling Hilary', and in the subsequent ones, 'To Hilary again, with all my love'. That introduced a new element. Barton and Aurelia's had always been hailed as the great example of a show business marriage that remained faithful, and yet who was this Hilary to whom he had dedicated five books? Charles knew he would have to find that out.

But for the moment he was more concerned with the deaths. They were easily found. Barton Rivers, in the guise of R.Q. Wilberforce, wrote his books to an unerring formula. In Chapter One, Maltravers Ratcliffe would return to his wife, Eithne, from some gallant exploit, and they would decide to go away somewhere to escape all thoughts of crime. In Chapter Two they would arrive at their destination, and, on the last page of the chapter, someone would die. Maybe this total predictability was one of the reasons why R.Q. Wilberforce couldn't find a publisher and had to produce the books himself.

The murders made fascinating reading. In *Death Takes A Tumble,* the victim apparently fell from a fire escape on the tower of a baronial castle. In *Death Takes A Wrong Turning* a rock, cunningly placed round a hairpin bend in the Dolomites, caused a young playboy to drive his Hispano-Suiza to destruction down the face of a cliff. In *Death Takes A Drive* the victim was run down by a Bentley that didn't stop (thus causing, because of the make of car, suspicion to fall on the spotless Maltravers Ratcliffe). And in *Death Takes a Stand* a young man in a stately home was killed by the apparently accidental fall of a heavy wall-mounted light-stand.

In each book the manner of the death was, either punningly or directly, suggested in the title.

And, in every case, whoever had actually committed the crime, behind it, masterminding the operation, had been 'the evil genius of von Strutter' (usually followed by an exclamation mark!).

And so, in these old blue volumes were prefigured the deaths of Sadie Wainwright, Scott Newton, Rod Tisdale and Robin Laughton. Their individual identity had not been important; so long as they were connected with the series called *The Strutters* they had earned the right to die.

Charles returned the four volumes to their shelf long before Stanley Harvey's deadline. He didn't look at *Death Takes a Short Cut.* He knew what happened in that one.

Someone got impaled on a Japanese samurai sword.

CHAPTER SIXTEEN

The tower block of W.E.T. House looked unchanged, modern, impassive, but internally it was crippled. There was no canteen or bar service, the security men's go-slow continued and members of other unions formed little mumbling groups. The company was like a very old man's body, in which no one knew which organ would fail next. Senior management sat like anxious doctors in their offices, waiting for the loudspeaker announcement or phone call that would signal the end, or at least the lapse into coma, of their patient.

But Peter Lipscombe was not the man to let that sort of atmosphere get him down. With Boy Scout brightness he welcomed each member of *The Strutters* cast into the building, and assured them all that everything was okay.

And so indeed it seemed. Costumes were laid in dressing-rooms, make-up girls waited to administer their tantalisingly short caresses, cameramen and sound-boom operators drifted towards the studio, Vision Mixer and PA to the control box, Sound and Vision Controllers to their adjacent stations. The set was up, and there seemed to be no reason why the rehearse/recording of Episode Eight of *The Strutters* should not start on camera at ten o'clock as scheduled.

Charles Paris wasn't there on the dot of ten, because, from force of habit, he had gone to the big Studio A, where Wragg and Bowen were having an uphill struggle with new directors and scriptwriters, and beginning to question the wisdom of their hugely expensive transfer from the BBC. (Why did they think they could change the inalienable law of television — that no comedy star was ever improved by moving from the BBC to ITV, and that for most a commercial offer was a sure sign that they had passed their peak of popularity?)

Charles realised his mistake as soon as he saw the

set of garish tinsel and dangling silver bicycle wheels. As he turned to leave, he nearly bumped into a familiar, and not unattractive, figure. 'Jay!'

'Actually, I call myself Jan Lewis now. It looks better on the roller caption.'

'Uh-huh. Well, how are things?'

'Fine. This Wragg and Bowen show is so complicated. There's lots to learn.'

'I'm sure.'

'Did you hear what happened yesterday?'

'Don't think so.'

'Oh, it was an absolute *disaster*. You know, this programme for the elderly . . .'

Oh yes, the Franchise-Grabber. He nodded.

'Well, you know they'd got this wonderful old boy in to front it. Ian Reynolds, he's nearly eighty.'

'Yes, I had heard.' A few times.

'Well, yesterday was their first day in the studio and when he got in front of the cameras — he dropped dead.'

'Oh dear.'

'Yes, they lost the whole studio day.'

Charles tut-tutted appropriately.

'They're going to get Robert Carton in instead. I'm sure he'll do it awfully well.'

'Oh, I should think so.' There was a silence. 'It'd be nice for us to get together again soon . . .'

'Charles!' She looked at him as if he had made an improper suggestion. Which indeed he had. But not one that had worried her before.

'What's the matter?'

'But, Charles, I'm on a different *programme* now.'

His dilatoriness in getting to Studio B didn't matter. He had checked with Mort Verdon, who assured him that the samurai sword would be kept locked in the prop store until required for the final scene. 'Can't leave things like that lying around, boofle. For a start, it's worth a few bob, and things have been known to disappear, you know . . . Also, it's an extremely businesslike weapon, dear. Very sharp. If somebody started fooling about with that, there could be a very sudden influx of new members to the Treble Section . . .'

Maybe Mort Verdon's protective eye would be sufficient to ward off any 'accidents', but Charles knew Barton Rivers was cunning in his madness, and didn't feel confident. As soon as the sword appeared on the set, he would watch Barton Rivers's every move. Any attempt to touch it and he'd pounce. He needed evidence to ensure that the old maniac was put away where he belonged. But he'd have to be quick. He wanted evidence, but he didn't want another corpse.

Studio B, when he found it, looked quite a bit smaller than Studio A, but he was informed that it had the same floor area. The difference was that the larger studio had permanent audience seats, while when Studio B had audience shows, banks of seats were brought in, thus reducing the acting area. The seating was built *in situ* on frames of bolted metal sections, and stood up in great wedges away from the studio back wall. (A large gap had to be left between this wall and the back of the bank of seats because of fire regulations.)

Charles slouched in the front row and watched the recording with mild interest. The atmosphere was different to the usual studio day. Normally the tension mounted as the day went on, building to the mock-climax of the Dress Run, and then the final release of the end of the recording. On the revised schedule, each scene was rehearsed until satisfactory, and then recorded. It made everyone more relaxed. In spite of the industrial stormclouds outside, in the studio all was cosy. Many of the actors commented how much they'd rather rehearse/record the show every week, forget the moribund studio audience and either dub on the laughs or — heretical thought to any traditional Light Entertainment mind! — dispense with them altogether.

Peter Lipscombe explained at considerable length how much more expensive this would be because of the cost of VTR machine time, but soon lost his audience in a welter of budgetary jargon.

Through the slow processes of the morning Charles kept an eye on Barton Rivers. The old man sat in the audience grinning inanely and watching the every move of his wife. Whatever had happened to his mind, his devotion to Aurelia seemed absolutely genuine, a devotion

161

reflected in such overblown and dated terms by the relationship between Maltravers and Eithne Ratcliffe.

Once again Charles wondered who on earth Hilary could be and where she fitted into the bizarre picture.

At one point he chatted to Barton. The old man, with his zany politeness, used a lot of 'dear boys', commented that doing the show this way was 'a rummy business' and asked Charles what chance he thought our chaps had against the Indians at the Oval.

Now that he had the key, Charles could hear the intonations of Maltravers Ratcliffe in every word. And, remembering the photograph of the fine young man in the Bentley, he could see that, if ever the filming of *Death Takes A Short Cut* had been feasible, Barton Rivers would have been ideal casting for it.

He contemplated challenging the old man with all he knew, but he didn't think it would work. The ruined mind would not be able to respond. No, he had to wait for the sword and see what happened.

They proceeded quickly on the new schedule and by lunchtime had recorded the bulk of the show. Of course, there were no canteen facilities, but Peter Lipscombe demonstrated that he did have his uses by laying on large supplies of take-away food in the dressing rooms. Mort Verdon was of the pessimistic opinion that this might be construed as strike-breaking and twitched visibly every time there was an announcement on the loudspeakers.

There were quite a few announcements on the loud-speakers that lunchtime, calling meetings of various branches of various unions, but, remarkably, the entire studio crew reassembled to continue work at two o'clock.

Charles began to feel nervous as the final scene of the episode drew near. He was taking a terrible risk. If something went wrong, another person could die.

Perhaps he should have gone to the police. But even as the idea came to him, he dismissed it. His story was so fanciful, so ridiculous, that no one would believe him. He remembered from his interview after the night's filming in Clapham how little the police cared for the romantic notions of amateurs.

The recording continued. The penultimate scene was

completed and the set had to be redressed before the final one, in which Colonel Strutter's Japanese neighbour was to present him with a samurai sword.

Dob Howarth, whose work for the day was finished, came into the audience, yawning. She smiled at Charles, giving him once again the full beam of her eyes. 'Oh, I think we'll get it all in the can now.'

'Looks like it.'

'I'm exhausted. Come and sit with me and tell me sweet stories, darling.'

Charles was torn. Barton Rivers sat two rows in front of him and he wanted to keep within range of the old man. Equally, he didn't want to arouse Aurelia's suspicions by not accompanying her up to the back of the audience seats.

It'd be all right. The sword wasn't even on the set yet. And it would only take a second to get down on stage. He moved up to join Aurelia in the back row.

'Be a relief when all this industrial trouble's over, won't it, Dob?'

'Will rather, darling. I must say it doesn't make the whole process any less tiring.'

Her voice was intimate and close. He decided to talk to her about Barton. She must know a bit of what was going on. Maybe, if he told her all of it, she would agree to having the old man put away. It could all be sorted out without further risk.

Charles put his arm along the back rail of the audience seating and asked gently, 'How *is* Barton, Dob?'

She sighed. 'Not getting better, I'm afraid.'

Charles looked down on to the set. Mort Verdon walked into the light bearing, like Miss World with her sceptre, the samurai sword.

Six rows down, the long figure of Barton Rivers rose to his feet.

Immediately, Charles did the same and started down the steps.

But Barton didn't go for the sword. Instead, with his fixed gentlemanly grin, he came up towards them.

Charles subsided back into his seat with relief. The danger had passed for the time being.

'Barton's mind works strangely, doesn't it, Dob?'

he murmured.

She sighed. 'I'm afraid so, darling.'

There was a sudden commotion on the set. Charles tensed, but Barton Rivers was still moving away from the sword.

Everyone seemed to be flooding into the studio looking bewildered. At last Bob Tomlinson emerged from the melee. He turned to the audience seats and shouted in his coster's voice, 'That's it, folks. A.C.T.T. has called a strike. We're all out. It's over.'

Then everything happened fast. Charles saw Mort Verdon put the samurai sword down on the sofa. Barton Rivers, who was now almost at the top of the audience steps, turned back towards the set.

But as Charles rose, the old man's arm suddenly swung round and caught him in the chest, toppling him backwards.

As the rail behind him gave way and Charles felt himself falling, falling backwards, his last thought was that he wished he'd read *Death Takes A Back Seat*.

CHAPTER SEVENTEEN

He landed with a terrible jolt that rearranged every cell in his body. He was winded and may have passed out for a few moments. Time seemed to have elapsed when he became aware of his surroundings.

Two men in lumberjack checked shirts lay on the studio floor with him. Both looked dazed and were rubbing various of their extremities. Around the three prone figures a little semi-circle of technicians had gathered.

One of the men on the floor found his tongue. 'Bloody strike-breaker,' he grumbled. 'Where the hell did you come from.

Charles pointed weakly up to the top of the bank of seats, where the back rail hung loose and the outline of his tipped-up seat showed.

'You're bloody lucky we're not seriously injured,' continued the man in the lumberjack checked shirt.

'Bloody lucky.'

'He didn't fall on purpose,' a voice said defensively.

'Comes to the same thing whether he did or didn't. Falling down on top of union members — that's the sort of thing that could cause a strike.'

'But we're already on strike.'

'Oh yes. Bloody lucky for him we are.'

The other lumberjack checked shirt groaned.

''Ere, you all right?' asked his mate.

The only reply he got was another groan.

The speaking shirt turned accusingly to Charles. ''Ere, you really hurt him. I reckon falling actors comes under industrial accident. We'll take the company for a lot of insurance on this.'

That thought seemed to make his own injuries worse, and he too groaned.

'You've chosen a bad time for that,' observed one of the watching cameramen. 'Now we're on strike, the company's not liable. In fact, with the security men on total strike, even the building isn't insured.'

'Bloody hell.' Both the lumberjack checked shirts stopped groaning, stood up, and walked off, grumbling.

Charles lay still. He didn't know if it was shock or genuine injury, but he felt numb, unable to move. There was no pain, just a lassitude, an unwillingness to come back to the real world.

He vaguely heard voices asking if he was all right and vaguely felt hands lifting him. With infinite caution, he put his weight on first one foot, then the other.

'Are you sure you're all right?' He focused on the anxious face of a young cameraman. 'There should be a nurse on duty in the building. I don't know if she'll have gone on strike yet. I could ring. I think the phones are still working.'

Slowly, Charles's faculties were coming back to him. He tried his voice and it seemed to work. 'No, no, I think I'm all right. Just shock, really. And I feel as if I'm a bit bruised. Let me go. I'll see if I can walk.'

He could. Just. It hurt. The feeling had come back to his body as well as his mind.

'Thank you. Thank you very much. I'll be okay.'

'Are you sure?'

'Yes. Thanks.'

He moved very slowly out of the studio. Each footstep, however gently he tried to place it, he jarred his back, and he felt himself sweating with the pain.

But he had no doubt about what he had to do. Or where he had to go. With pain, but determination, he moved slowly towards Dressing Room Number One, which had been allocated by *The Strutters* new PA to Aurelia Howarth.

He knocked, and her husky, cultivated voice gave him permission to enter.

She was sitting at the mirror adjusting her make-up. Her usual diaphanous gowns and the ones she wore for the show were so similar that he couldn't tell whether she had changed or not.

Barton Rivers was not there.

Charles's appearance shocked her. 'You survived,' she gasped.

He nodded, which he found a rather painful action.

Aurelia seemed to be in the grip of a strong emotion and it was a moment before she managed to murmur, 'Thank God.'

'Yes, I survived. Unlike Sadie and Scott and Robin.'

Tears glinted in the huge unfocused eyes. 'I'm so sorry. I kept thinking he'd stop.'

'*Death Takes a Back Seat*,' said Charles. 'I never got to read that one.'

She looked at him with surprise, but also a touch of relief, relief perhaps that now her terrible secret was shared. 'So you worked it out from the books?'

'Yes. But I was stupid today. I kept thinking it'd be the samurai sword.'

She gave a strained smile. 'Of course. *Death Takes A Short Cut*. I'm afraid I'd given up trying to work out what would happen next. I just kept praying it would all stop, but it went on, and on.'

'He'll have to be put away,' Charles said gently.

Aurelia inclined her head. 'I suppose so. That's what I feared. That's why — once I knew — all I could do was beg him to stop. I couldn't actually betray him. Not my husband.'

'No.' Charles felt the stirring of a deep emotion, sympathy for her pain. 'But why? I see that he was following the murders in the books, but he must have had some reason, some logic, however bizarre.'

Aurelia Howarth shrugged. 'Barton just said it had to be done. He said that von Strutter was the mastermind behind every evil and the series of *The Strutters* was part of a plot to take over the country.'

'But in the books it's von Strutter who commits the crimes, not Maltravers Ratcliffe.'

There was a little humourless laugh. 'It'd be funny if it weren't so tragic. Barton said that the only way to counter the Teutonic devil's schemes was to use his own methods.'

'I see.' Yes, in the mind of a madman, that was a kind of logic. 'How long has he been like this?'

Strangely, as he said it, the line seemed to echo Claudius' response to the demented Ophelia, 'How long hath she been thus?'

Aurelia sighed. 'It was the war. The War left many scars, and the worst of them were invisible. For Barton, it destroyed everything. First, there was the film of *Death Takes A Short Cut*. That had been set up with great difficulty, with a great deal of money, but it promised so well. It would have been the two of us working together, as equals, working on scripts from his book. Barton hoped it would be the first of a series of films and would make his career. But it was cancelled as soon as war was declared. So the war, the Germans, to Barton's mind von Strutter, ruined that chance.

'And he wasn't even allowed to revenge the affront personally. He was turned down for active service because he was too old. I went off to entertain the troops all over the place, and once again Barton was left behind.

'But that was not the worst . . .' Aurelia's voice broke, but she regained control quickly. 'Our son was of an age to fight for his country. In January 1944, we heard that he had been killed on active service.'

'Your son's name was Hilary?'

She nodded, unable for a moment to speak. Charles waited until she could continue.

'From that time on, Barton was changed. He stopped

writing, said that he would never write again. And he started to get ideas, strange, grotesque ideas. He started to dress and talk like this character and to plan revenge on von Strutter. At first he was convinced that Hitler was von Strutter in disguise, and that he would win the war and we would be overrun by the Germans.'

'His mind went?'

She nodded again, very slowly. 'But I always thought he was harmless. And then . . . this started. At first I couldn't believe it was true, then I just hoped it would stop. Now I still wish it could be kept secret. But you've worked it all out . . .' Her hands dropped helplessly on to her lap.

So there it was. Bizarre, yes, ridiculous, yes, but true. Charles' grotesque theory had been proved correct. He felt a slight dissatisfaction. He'd never like the idea of psychopathic murders; always felt more comfortable with a logic of motivation he could understand. Still, Barton Rivers was his culprit, and Barton Rivers had to be found. One crime, the murder from *Death Takes A Short Cut*, had not yet been recreated.

'Where is Barton now, Dob?'

'In the building. Not far away.' She spoke distractedly.

'He must be found.'

'Yes.' A listless monosyllable. Then, in a different tone, 'I still think it's remakable how you worked it out. I suppose you saw the books in Peter's office.'

'In Peter's office?'

'Yes. You know I lent them to him. Barton gave me a set years ago, and forgot about them when he threw out all his copies.'

'Those were the books you thought might make a series?'

'Yes.'

Charles felt a great surge of excitement. Something had happened. He hadn't worked it out in detail yet, but his mind was suddenly racing away in a new direction.

He looked piercingly at Aurelia. 'I don't believe you.'

'What on earth do you mean?'

He thought out loud, piecing it together as he went along. 'Those books would never make a telvision series.'

'That's a matter of opinion,' she said frostily.

'No, it's not, it's a matter of fact. They would have

168

made a pretty peculiar set of films in the 1940s, but a television series in 1979 — never.'

'Perhaps not. I just thought, hoped that —'

'No, you didn't. The idea is a bummer and you know it.'

'I don't understand.'

'Yes, you do. If there's one quality which has distinguished every moment of your career, it's your judgement. You have always done the right thing, chosen the right show, the right part. You know what works and what doesn't.'

'Perhaps I did once, but as we get older, our judgement gets less reliable.'

'Your judgement is as good as it has ever been. And yet I heard you say to Peter Lipscombe on two occasions that you thought those books would make a good television series. I didn't know what the books in question were at that stage or I'd have smelt a rat earlier.'

'I don't know what you mean.'

'Nor do I completely, but I'm getting there.' Charles paused and built his thoughts up slowly. 'You knew, of course you knew, that those books had no potential at all for television and yet you still very deliberately brought them to Peter Lipscombe's attention. Why? I think you wanted them read, you wanted someone to see the parallels with the crimes that surrounded the *Strutters* series. Yes, in spite of what you say about wanting to keep your husband's crimes quiet, I think you were deliberately trying to draw attention to the books' parallels with what he was doing. And, if you'd given them to anyone other than a television producer, the connection might have been made a lot earlier.'

Aurelia looked crestfallen. 'All right, so what if I did? I couldn't actually betray Barton, but by offering the books I was at least opening up the possibility that someone might work out what was happening.'

Charles was almost seduced by her meekness, but not quite. 'If that was the case, why didn't you offer more help, show the books to the police or something, tell someone? And why did you sound so disappointed when I said I'd worked out the connection just now?'

Aurelia now looked angry. 'You're talking nonsense.

169

Charles. Why else would I lend the books?'

He looked at her very straight. 'I think you lent them as an insurance policy. So that they were there if anyone started connecting the deaths. And so that if suspicion started to move towards you, it could be diverted towards Barton.'

He wasn't sure, but he knew that he had to hold her stare until she gave way if he was to have any chance of finding out the truth.

It took a long time, but eventually she lowered her eyes. 'So . . . it's confession time, is it?'

'I think so.' With caution and discomfort, Charles sat down. 'You killed Sadie Wainwright?'

'It was an accident. Really, an accident.' The wonderful blue eyes looked totally sincere, but Charles was getting suspicious of their messages. 'It was a stupid thing. She had been being unpleasant about Cocky all day, really offensive. Then, when we were walking up the fire escape she said something even viler and I lost my temper I pushed her and the railing gave way. That is the truth.'

'So Cocky *was* the motivation?'

'Yes. And after that night's filming, I thought you'd worked it out. That's why I poisoned him.'

'Poisoned Cocky?'

She nodded. 'I thought if you saw how little I was affected by his death, you'd discount him as a motive against Sadie. But then Romney came along with his wretched card and I broke down, so it . . .'

Charles tried to slow things down, so that his mind could accommodate the new information. 'Okay. Sadie's death you say was an accident . . . ?'

'Yes, and she was such a peculiarly unlovely person I can't think that anyone was too upset by it.' She spoke with a kind of blind selfishness, the murderer's immunity to other people's existence. 'Anyway, I didn't want investigations and things. I had my image to think of.' Image — the star's eternal motivation. Was the perfect marriage to Barton just another reflection of the image?

Charles nudged on. 'But Sadie's wasn't the only death.'

'No. As I say, she was an accident, really. I thought she would soon be forgotten, but . . .'

A new set of facts fell into place. Scott Newton had

170

been in a terrible state after the recording of the *Strutters* pilot, Scott Newton had wanted a private word with Aurelia at the first readthrough, Scott Newton had been suddenly affluent at the filming at Bernard Walton's house. 'But,' suggested Charles, 'Scott Newton had seen Sadie die and, being under a certain amount of financial pressure, had started to blackmail you.'

Aurelia nodded. 'I gave him one big pay-off, but he wasn't going to be satisfied with that. So he had to go.' It was said very matter-of-fact.

'You moved the flower-urn yourself?'

'Barton did it.'

'You told him all about the —'

She laughed unattractively. 'I told him that Scott was one of von Strutter's spies, and that we had to destroy him. And I said the only way we could thwart the Teutonic devil was to use his own murder methods. The way Sadie died had been a coincidence, but I suddenly saw that it could fit very conveniently into a pattern.'

'And Barton didn't question what you were suggesting?'

'Not at all. He took to it instantly. It was what he'd been waiting for all his life, for someone to share his delusions.' She spoke of her husband as one might of a large and inconvenient pet.

'And it was after Scott's death that you gave Peter Lipscombe the books, so that he could make the connection between the two crimes if he chose to?'

'Yes. He mentioned the possibility of their being connected in one of his little notes and that got me worried.'

'And, if they ever were discovered, you'd set it up so that Barton would get the blame.'

'He'd never betray me. Never betray a *lady*,' she said dismissively.

Charles sighed. 'That still doesn't explain the deaths of Rod Tisdale and Robin Laughton.'

'No,' Aurelia agreed. 'It doesn't.' She let out a sudden peal of laughter. It was a famous sound, a sound that had been heard on millions of recordings of *I Dream of Dancing*, but at this moment its gaiety was not infectious. 'I'm afraid I was hoist with my own petard.'

'What do you mean?'

'I am afraid I had planted the idea of a von Strutter

171

conspiracy rather too firmly in my poor husband's head. He started recreating the other murders completely off his own bat. Obviously what I had asked him to do had struck a chord. Barton was happy, happier than he had ever been. I think he felt that murder was going to be the one thing in his life that he had ever been good at.'

'So you had nothing to do with the last two deaths?'

'Nothing at all. Mind you, they were not without convenience. They shifted suspicion from me. The death of that tiresome Floor Manager put you off the scent, for a start.'

She smiled. It was the same famous smile, but its charm had gone. Charles recoiled from the image of this woman playing on her husband's illness, winding him up like some demented clockwork mouse to the random murders of people she regarded as irrelevant. That was it, he realised — through all the charm, she had never recognised the relevance of anyone in the world but herself. Perhaps, given more understanding, more care from his wife, Barton's descent into insanity could have been checked.

But it wasn't the moment for conjecture. 'And Barton's attack on me — was that just random?'

She shook her head slowly, with another little smile. 'No, I'm afraid that was my suggestion. I planted the idea, I have to confess. Your inquisitiveness was becoming rather disturbing, and I saw a good way of satisfying my husband's lunacy and removing a danger to me.'

'I'm honoured.'

'Yes.' She paused. 'Now, of course, you represent even more of a danger to me.' She looked at her watch and Charles realised why she had vouchsafed him this long confession. She had been playing for time, awaiting the return of her demented assassin.

The door opened, and Barton Rivers entered with his customary idiotic gallantry. He seemed totally unsurprised to see Charles. 'Bung-ho, old boy,' he said. 'Lovely weather for it.'

'Barton,' commanded Dame Aurelia Howarth, 'Mr Paris is being rather tiresome.'

The death's head turned to face him. 'I say, old boy. Mustn't worry the little lady. Perhaps you ought to be off.'

'I didn't mean that, Barton,' she snapped. 'I mean, get rid of him.'

'Eh?'

'He's one of von Strutter's spies.'

'Oh, can't have that, eh? Don't understand the rules of cricket, that lot.'

'Kill him, Barton!'

The old man stepped forward, the claws shot out and Charles felt himself lifted out of his chair. The strength was enormous and terrifying. His arms were clamped to his sides and, in his weakened state, he was unable to move.

The eyes in the skull-face glinted at him, horribly close.

But then they seemed to lose focus, to waver, and change to the confused eyes of a senile old man.

'Difficult, you know, old girl,' said Barton. 'Only one of the Teutonic devil's tricks we haven't used is the old samurai sword, and I'm afraid I haven't got one of those on me.'

'It doesn't matter how it's done,' Dame Aurelia Howarth hissed.

But she was up against the unassailable logic of lunacy. 'Oh, but it does, old thing. There's a right way and a wrong way, you know.'

'Just kill him!'

'Have to find a sword first, my angel. Have to think. I wonder if there's anything else we could do, or has von Strutter finally triumphed?'

Charles Paris felt very tired, while this surreal discussion about his death went on. He wanted to laugh, but hadn't got the energy.

Then the door opened again and he looked up with relief to see the startled face of Mort Verdon. 'Oops, sorry, boofles. Thought you'd all gone.'

Barton Rivers did not appear to notice the new arrival, but relaxed his hold on his victim's arms. Aurelia fixed Charles with an expression of hatred, but seemed to recognise that nothing could be done with Mort there. 'Come on, Barton.'

The living skeleton did not react.

'Maltravers,' she murmured.

He came to life. He gave her a gallant little bow, and

offered his arm. 'Of course, Eithne, my angel. We'll soon get this ghastly business sorted out.'

She took his arm almost reluctantly. She seemed hypnotised by him, half-attracted, half-repelled. And there was something else in her look, which with a shock Charles recognised as fear. As Barton led his wife out of the dressing room door, he seemed very much in command of their relationship.

'Come, let's away, my fair one, and we'll be there in two twos.'

Relief, and the expression of amazement on Mort Verdon's face, reduced Charles to helpless laughter. As amazement changed to concern, he realised he was hysterical.

'Oh God,' he finally managed to say, 'I've never been so glad to see anyone.'

Mort Verdon flicked an eyebrow with his little finger. 'I bet you say that to all the boys.'

Charles giggled again and then sobered up. 'You look a worried man, Mort.'

'I am, boofle, I am.'

'Why?'

'Always the same when you've got something valuable in the studio. It gets nicked.'

'What are you talking about?'

'The samurai sword has completely disappeared, dear. Completely.'

Oh, my God!' Charles realised that his ordeal was not yet over.

'That's why I'm going round the dressing rooms and —'

'Mort,' said Charles.

'Yes, dear.'

'Would you mind walking out with me?'

Mort Verdon's eyebrows shot up. 'Well now,' he said, 'there's a novelty!'

There was no sign of the Bentley or its owners as they left the dead stillness of W.E.T. House, but a cruising taxi was passing and Charles hailed it. He'd feel safer inside than exposed on the streets.

He was going to give the Hereford Road address, but suddenly panicked that Aurelia might know it. He felt certain they'd be out to get him, but he didn't know how. Perhaps there would be a clue in the R.Q. Wilberforce books. He asked the driver to take him to Hampstead.

Stanley Harvey objected that it was very inconvenient and ill-mannered, but Charles was in no mood to be stopped. He bulldozed his way into the little man's library and flicked quickly through *Death Takes A Short Cut*.

It was unhelpful. Then Charles remembered Stanley Harvey had mentioned some other R.Q. Wilberforce papers in the filing cabinet, and he demanded to see them.

It was the only thing he could think of. Perhaps there would be some further clue, some pointer that might help him avert the final tragedy.

With bad grace, Stanley Harvey opened the filing cabinet.

Charles riffled through the piles of manuscript and letters at speed, not certain what he was looking for, but convinced that there must be something.

In a few minutes he found it. A pointer, yes, but it didn't point in the way he had expected.

There was just one sheet. It was headed as if it were the start of a new book, but at the bottom of the page, a thick line had been ruled. All that was written below that was the date, 30th January 1944.

CHAPTER ONE
THE TRIUMPH OF EVIL

Maltravers Ratcliffe looked at his wife as he put down the 'phone, and felt the glow of wonder and gratitude that her visage always aroused in him. The golden hair! The heavenly blue eyes, more precious than a Rajah's treasure store! Eithne's small face was set in the lines of courage, as together they listened to the distant, ominous boom of the guns.

'London has fallen, my angel,' he announced with his same old debonair carelessness.

She gasped; though it was the news that she had feared, to hear it confirmed was still a profound shock to her sensibilities.

'So von Strutter has triumphed!'

'Triumphed over this sceptred isle,' her husband rejoined with the spirit, 'but never over Maltravers Ratcliffe!'

'It is inevitable that the Teutonic devil will seek you out to exact his ghastly revenge.'

'Inevitable,' he confirmed. 'But let him seek! To seek is not to find! Come, my angel, we will go for a drive! Tell

by R.Q. WILBERFORCE

Wallace to provide a luncheon-basket and tog up in your gladdest rags!'

They drove towards the South. The Bentley swallowed the miles keenly, relishing the open road. Never had the garden of England looked more beauteous! Never had Maltravers and Eithne Ratcliffe been so much together, so equal in their love! They took their luncheon in a flowery dell and chattered amiably of cricket and of their happiness.

Then the great Bentley, smoothly seeming to sense its destination, headed towards the sea, towards those white cliffs which, until this last devil, had hitherto daunted every foreign invader.

As they neared the cliff-top, Maltravers Ratcliffe, without diminishing the great car's speed, took his wife's small hand in his. 'Take heart, my angel!' he cried cheerily. 'We may thank our stars that we have had each other. Onward now, my fair one — and we'll be there in two twos!'

The news of Aurelia Howarth and Barton Rivers's fatal car crash was on the radio the following morning. It wasn't the first item. That was of course the ITV strike.

CHAPTER EIGHTEEN

DAME AURELIA HOWARTH

The death of Aurelia Howarth, who died in a car accident together with her husband, Barton Rivers, robs the British theatre of one of its most glittering and best-loved stars. Born Anne Howarth, she was the daughter of a grocer and spent her early years near Guildford. Her great natural talents led to her enrolment in the stage school from where she progressed to the chorus of a West End revue, *Careless Rapture*, at the tender age of fifteen. She was 'spotted' in this show by the Great Andre Charlot, who gave her solo spots in some of his revues, and later taken up by the impresario C.B. Cochran, one of the most famous of whose 'Young Ladies' she became. Her biggest successes of this period were in *Parisian Trifles*, *Only the Night* and *Shimmering Stars*. It was in this last show that she first sang *I Dream of Dancing*, the song that she made her own and which virtually became her signature tune. She also went with *Shimmering Stars* to Broadway where, under the title of *Box of Tricks*, it became one of the hits of the season, and established Aurelia Howarth as an important new star in America. During the Thirties she played leading roles in many British films, of which the most memorable are probably *Lovers' Moon*, *Princess of Dreams* and *Tomorrow's Gone*. During the War she worked indefatigably entertaining the troops, services which were recognised by a CBE in 1947. In the post-war years her career took a new turn and she started to build a reputation as a straight actress. Long runs in the West End in such shows as *The Long Climb*, *Here We Go A-Wassailing* and *The Former Mrs Wellington* demonstrated her versatility. Then, at an age when many people contemplate retiring, Aurelia Howarth started to work in the growing medium of television, where she proved very popular, particularly in the role of the scatty Mrs Strutter in the comedy series, *What'll The Neighbours Say?* She was working on a new series in the same character at the time of her death. Throughout a long career in the theatre, Aurelia Howarth was one of the few performers who commanded universal love and who never did a malicious action to anyone. Both in the profession and with the public, her popularity never waned. She was created a Dame of the British Empire in the recent Birthday Honours List. She married Barton Rivers, a revue performer, in 1918 and their one son, Hilary, was killed in action in 1944.

There was no separate obituary for Barton Rivers. Neither his reputation as an actor nor as a writer justified it.

Charles Paris tried ringing his wife Frances on and off for about three days and, when he still didn't get any reply, he rang their daughter Juliet at her home in Pangbourne.

'No, Mummy's not there at the moment.'

'Where is she?'

'It's school holidays. She's away.'

'Where?'

'Naxos.'

'That's Greece, isn't it?'

'One of the islands, yes.'

'Do you happen to know if she went on her own or . . . ?'

'She went with a friend.'

'You don't know who?'

'No.'

'Oh.'

'She'll be back in about ten days.'

'Ah. I'll ring her then. How are things with you?'

'Oh fine. Hectic with the twins.'

'I'm sure.'

'Still, they start play school in September. And I'm going back to work. Just mornings.

'Ah.'

'Miles and I would love to see you if you're free. Give us a buzz if you're about.'

'Yes, I will.'

'I must dash. Damian's pulling Julian's hair. 'Bye.'

'Goodbye.'

West End Television Ltd,
W.E.T. House,
235—9 Lisson Avenue,
London NW1 3PQ.
29th October 1979.

Dear Charles,

Now that the strike's over and life here is getting back to normal, I wanted to drop you a note to thank you for all your hard work over the series of *The Strutters*.

Obviously, with Dob's tragic death, there is no possibility of the series being completed. Recasting such a major role is out of the question. Still, you should by now, I hope, have received your outstanding contractual payments.

Plans here are still rather fluid, so the future of the programmes in the series that were completed is uncertain. There's still a bit of editing and sound-dubbing to do on them, and since the demand on those facilities here is pretty heavy at the moment, it'll be some time before they're ready to be transmitted. But the 'powers that be' have spoken of the possibility of putting the seven completed programmes out as a mini-series in the Spring or Summer. We'll have to see.

Now that we don't have *The Strutters* there's a possibility that we may do another series of *What'll The Neighbours Say?* at some point. Obviously, without Dob, it'll have to be rather different and so I can't really say whether your character would be likely to recur or not. Anyway, it's a long way in the future and will depend when Bernard Walton's free. He's currently in Australia doing a tax year (and, incidentally, remaking a *What'll The Neighbours Say* series out there with an Australian supporting cast!).

I haven't heard much from the *Strutters* crowd, though I did see George Birkitt with his wife at a premiere the other week. Oh, and also I have to pass on the bad news that Willy and Sam Tennison have split up. I've just had a very exciting new script from Willy, provisionally titled *Marriage on the Rocks*.

Once again, many thanks for all you did to make *The Strutters* what it was. I look forward to working with you again on some other project.

With the warmest good wishes,

Yours sincerely,

Peter

PETER LIPSCOMBE

Producer *The Strutters*

DANCE FOR DIPLOMATS

Palma Harcourt

'Palma Harcourt's novels are splendid' *Desmond Bagley*

Catherine Rayle, history don at Oxford, becomes Britain's first-ever woman permanent representative to NATO in Brussels. But her initial instinct to refuse the position was a good one, for Catherine gets drawn into a cloak-and-dagger world involving a defecting Russian ballet dancer; suddenly all are dancing, to a tune they have not called.

'The story unfolds with pace and excitement' *Evening News*

Futura Publications
Fiction/Thriller
0 7088 2573 7

MURDER IN THE TITLE

Simon Brett

'Mercilessly witty send-up of threadbare stage whodunnits'
Guardian

Playing the corpse in a wooden murder mystery at the Regent Theatre, Rugland Spa, is not exactly a triumph for Charles Paris, actor: in fact his career could hardly sink any lower.

But suddenly the mystery spilled over into real life when a bizarre sequence of events culminated in the Artistic Director's apparent suicide. And the talents of Charles Paris, amateur sleuth, were called into action.

'every page is gentle fun'
Daily Telegraph

'the sounds and smells, the ambitions and frustrations, of a provincial repertory company . . . a neat homicide, and an economic, uncontrived, satisfactory solution'
Financial Times

Futura Publications
Fiction/Crime
0 7088 2520 6

PEL AND THE BOMBERS

Mark Hebden

The majestically named Inspector Evariste Clovis Desiré Pel, policeman in the historic duchy of Burgundy, has plenty on his hands when five murders disturb his peaceful city on Bastille night. Evidently a terrorist group is preparing an explosive welcome for the President, due shortly on a State visit. Where will things end? Pel's wooing of the charming Mme Faivre-Perret and his running battle with his tyrannical landlady must be rudely interrupted while he tracks down the culprits.

'downbeat humour and some delightful dialogue'
Financial Times

'Mr Hebden has created a nice band of flics'
Oxford Times

Futura Publications
Fiction/Crime
0 7088 2487 0

A MORBID TASTE FOR BONES

Ellis Peters

In the twelfth-century Benedictine monastery of
Shrewsbury, Brother Cadfael has settled down to a
quiet life in charge of the herbarium after an
adventurous — and far from monastic — youth. But
when his prior determines to acquire the bones of a
saint from a remote Welsh village, Cadfael's worldly
experience becomes vitally important. It is fortunate
indeed that his skills as a herbalist are matched by his
prowess as a detective, since the obstacles to the
expedition include murder . . .

'gripping and knowledgeable, this shows yet again
Miss Peters's astonishing range'
Spectator

'soothing, but no shortage of mayhem'
Observer

Futura Publications
Fiction/Crime
0 7088 2552 4

All Futura Books are available at your bookshop or newsagent, or can be ordered from the following address:
Futura Books, Cash Sales Department,
P.O. Box 11, Falmouth, Cornwall

Please send cheque or postal order (no currency), and allow 55p for postage and packing for the first book plus 22p for the second book and 14p for each additional book ordered up to a maximum charge of £1.75 in U.K.

Customers in Eire and B.F.P.O. please allow 55p for the first book, 22p for the second book plus 14p per copy for the next 7 books, thereafter 8p per book.

Overseas customers please allow £1.00 for postage and packing for the first book and 25p per copy for each additional book.